PROVEN
by the
BIRTHMARK

WILLIEMAE LATIMORE

Proven by the Birthmark

Copyright © 2024 by Williemae Latimore

ISBN: 979-8895310601 (sc)

ISBN: 979-8895310618 (e)

Writers' Branding
(877) 608-6550
www. writersbranding. com
media@writersbranding. com

CONTENTS

CHAPTER 1

Proven By The Birthmark is about a girl who was rejected by her father because he thought he was not her father. He was a very jealous man and accused his wife of any man who looked twice at her.

The child suffered much and was in and out of various foster care homes, some were good and caring, others were the pits, but she remained steadfast in her goals for life, did well in school. At an early age she felt that if she knew more about life it would help her, because from the experiences she was having, it did not seem like the right way she was being treated. She could not understand why she was not able to live at home and she was constantly being accused of things she did not do or ever thought of doing. There were times she was accused of things which happened when she was not at home. At school, was her only refuge where she had any say. She learned to solve many mathematical problems which seemed hard for other students. The teachers were pleased with her work and she at an early age would reach out and help other students.

Ruthie was sort of happy, in a way. She would be getting married the very next day to someone she was fond of but not truly in love with. Her wedding would consist of all the festivities that went along with weddings. The only difference was that she would not be dressed in white which symbolizes purity and virginity because she was married before.

Ruthie felt that part mattered very little because she felt pure inside and that's what counted.

Ruthie was forty years old now and was as attractive as any twenty-five year old simply because she took care of herself. Deep down she knew she still loved Troy and she believed Todd knew it, but he cared enough to want her as his wife anyway. Todd was a loving kind hearted man, especially to a woman her age with six children who were very close to their father. She could not understand why her husband Troy chose to want a divorce, she never did anything wrong and as far as she knew he was not seeing any other woman. He still supported the children and came around to visit. She just felt that he no longer loved her and supposed things like that happen in relationships. She decided it was time for her to move along in her life. She did everything she knew to reach out to Troy but nothing seemed to make him want to return home to the family.

She had encountered many problems in the last two years, trying to work and raise their six children as well as trying to straighten out her alcoholic husband. She stood by him for the children's sake and because she loved him very much. He walked out on her and the children and kept bouncing back even after their divorce. She had to remind him that he requested the divorce and as a result, to her, that means that he no longer wanted her. Troy appeared to be very unsettled. However, Ruthie felt that she had to put a stop to him trying to use her as his wife. When her husband Troy's problem began to affect the children, she knew it was time to let go. Ruthie knew she had a job to do almost alone and work, education and good health was the only in road. She knew what alcohol could do to a person, so she stayed away from it. She knew what drugs could do in your life, so she stayed away from them as well. She could see how obesity could ruin your appearance, health and how others see you, so she controlled that aspect of her life which wasn't hard to do especially when you have to work, care for the family home, high school teens and keep others in college. Ruthie knew how important it was for children to have some sort of parental foundation to stand on when they are growing up and to lean on for a while after they grow up, until they can get their bearings. She wanted to make sure her and Troy's children had this.

Ruthie knew Troy's parents never truly liked her but she remain respectful to them for Troy's sake. She never did anything out-of-the -way to them. She always tried to overlook any disrespectful comments they made around her. One thing she knew was that they wanted Troy to marry her friend's daughter who had no interest in Troy. The Woodland family felt that they were the "Pillow of the Community" or I might say "Better than anyone else" Their daughter Katrina was very nice and did not feel the way they did. She struggled to get by in school. In Katrina's Junior year in High School they made contact with Ruthie, through a friend that knew her to help Katrina to bring up her grades. When Ruthie was almost ready to graduate High School they offered her a place to stay with them. She refused because she had enough of living with others she wanted a place of her own.

The Woodland's were very upset and embarrassed when Katrina returned from college after her first semester Married and expecting her first child. That sort of calm them down a bit.

Ruthie loved Troy very much, in fact, she refused to rush into marriage to Doctor Todd Raine because she was a little unsure of herself. She still had strong feelings for Troy.

They had experienced a breakdown in their marriage and could no longer talk. Troy's struggle was between alcohol, his parents, wife and children. The alcohol and parents won.

●▪▪▪▪▪▪▪▪▪▪▪▪▪▪▪▪▪▪▪▪▪▪▪▪▪▪▪▪●

Ruthie thought back through her life and what had brought her to this day. The pressures she faced at an early age was astronomical. She remembered the attention which was given her sisters and brothers, as she was overlooked. When siblings ran into problems or injured themselves, they were pampered and when the same things happened to her she was considered clumsy. By the time she was seven years old, she was a complete outcast and was put up for adoption. She was considered a difficult child and her parents were unable to care for her. (Which was totally untrue, she never talked back, rarely asked for anything, except what came her way, when accused of anything, she would deny it without any other comment) When Ruthie was placed in Foster Care Home, it was with someone who had skills dealing with children having difficulty adjusting.

The Caseworker who had charge of Ruthie had a problem identifying the problem Ruthie's parents cited. As she questioned Ruthie, the more she felt it was the parents who had an adjustment problem, not the child. She thought it was best she was out of the home, especially when parents go to that extreme to be relieved of a child.

Most people take children in for monetary reasons and when they get tired of caring for them they send them.

Ruthie was bounced around to various Foster Care Homes, some were nice, others the pits. In some of the Foster Care Homes, they got extra privileges if they didn't tell what was going on in the house and how many people were there. Ruthie was a little "green" and the foster parent failed to educate her, so when the Caseworker questioned her she told the truth and they got in trouble.

Ruthie did well in school because she was moved around so much and didn't have time to make friends, so all her energy went into her studies. The few people her age she got to know had a fairly stable home life. They had mothers and fathers in the home and some sisters and brothers. Some of her foster care parents had stable families and she visited many times. She began to get an idea what her family would be like when she got married.

After about two years, Ruthie's parents were forced to take her back into their home. Soon after, her parents separated. Her mother became ill and passed away about two years later. All the children were placed in foster care until their father locate a place large enough for them. Somehow Ruthie's father managed to leave her where she was (in foster care). Without her he had one less child to care for.

When Ruthie was eleven years old, she was sent to live with an elderly couple who became quite fond and concerned about her welfare and not the money they received for her care. Ruthie did well in school and was well mannered and considerate.

Her youthful experience in life had taught her that the smarter you are, respectful, well mannered and resourceful the better you will get along with others. She had learned to deal with most situations at her age.

The Carters did not have any children. The ones they had, had some sort of strange illness and lived only for a short while after birth. The Carters had a lot of love to share and Ruthie was on the receiving end for three years. During that period, Ruthie excelled in school. She took voice lessons, piano and Mrs Carters taught her how to make her own clothes. Her time was filled with education in various things.

The Carters got Ruthie involved in their church. She became a little leader. She learned how to become a young leader in many areas of the church. She developed the youth Choir and because of her outgoing abilities she began to draw many of the other youth to join. She developed a Youth Activity club which helped children with their school work and was teaching them all she was learning how to play the piano. She was smart and caught on fast and was a step above her teachers. She became a "shining star" the while she was with the Carters. The Carters were very smart people in the school system community and well known around the town. They purchased high quality things and paid their bills on time. They also reached out and helped others in need. They could be considered a few steps above middle class. The both of them earned a good salary for many years with no one to spend it on. They had a very lucrative savings account with no one to share it with. They took in Ruthie, not for the money, but only to find someone they feel they could help.

Unknown to Ruthie, all the money the Carters received for the care of Ruthie was placed in a savings account for her education.

They tried to adopt her but because of their age her father would not take the time to sign the papers because he felt that if they died they would probably make him take her in.

When everything was all set for him to sign the papers, he claimed he had some problem and could not leave home at the time. Another date was set and he had another excuse.

The Carter's still kept Ruthie and continued to treat her as if she was their own. In their hearts they felt that one day she would be their own.

In their hearts Ruthie became the child they never had and cherish. She was the child they felt was meant to be theirs. She was outgoing in a quiet way, she listened with all ears and followed directions without a lot of feedback. She was loving and kind to everyone. Easy to learn and willing to reach out in any time of need to anyone. Ruthie tend to stand firm on what she believe and what she was taught. If she had something she wanted to do and one disagree, she will fully explain her reasoning. She studied her bible religiously and was a believer in doing what is right. She treated everyone with respect. She understood much about life because of the way her parents and siblings treated her. They accused her of things she knew she was not guilty of, (her parents and her siblings). She felt that she would never be that way to anyone. Ruthie felt that she loved life and she wanted others to learn and love life as well and felt that she would never do anything to hurt anyone, if she could help it. She still did not understand why her parents did not want her. She knew she did not ever do the things they accused her of. She felt that one day she will find out why she was treated as an outcast, probably when she get older. Even her mother failed to stand up for her. She had so many why? ? One thing she knew was she was not a bad girl. She would never think to pour water in her sister's bed. Her sister, she knew, would wet the bad, but she never pointed out to her parents because she thought they knew. She was accused of getting in her sister's bed and wetting it because she was able to get to the toilet in time. Her bed was next to the bathroom, why would she walk across to her sister's bed when within a few steps she could be on the toilet. How could she make them understand? She was accused of breaking a window when all the windows were on the other side of the room. Her sister never allowed her to come on her side of the room.

Mrs Carter's sister died in Florida and Ruthie's piano recital was the same day. So Mrs Carter decided to go alone and leave Mr. Carter to take Ruthie to the recital. Anyway, she knew he knew more about music than she did. She would make excuses to her family for him..

On the flight home from Florida the plane crashed that Mrs. Carters was on. It took a while to recover all the bodies, identify them and get them to the families. Shortly after the funeral for Mrs Carters, Mr Carters had a massive heart attack and died instantly. Ruthie was devastated. She was so very much loved by the Carters and she loved them so desperately. After the initial shock was over, Ruthie did not want to go to another foster care home. She got in touch with her father in hopes that she could be with her sisters and brothers, but her father had not changed. He tried to cover himself by telling her that her older sister had married and tentatively moved out but was expected back along with her husband any time. He told her that her other sister was pregnant with no intentions of getting married and one brother was in some sort of trouble and wished she would stay where she was because he wanted no more headaches with teenagers. Ruthie tried to assure him that she would not be a problem, but that did not help--he still felt the same. At age fourteen, she had to contend with another set of foster parents or go back to the shelter which she hated.

Ruthie liked the freedom of foster care homes because they were not as strict as the shelter. Her next home was with a family who were much poorer than the State Child Placement Center knew about. At the Brenes, she got very little to eat and if she was late getting in, she soon realized, she got nothing at all. Ruthie stayed at school a lot for extra curricular activities and assistance in keeping her grades up. Her guidance counselor had worked it out with her caseworker and Mrs. Brenes before she was physically placed there. After it became almost unbearable, Ruthie discussed the conditions at the Brenes with her guidance counselor, but she explained to her that she wanted to stay there because if the caseworker knew what was going on, they would take her away and she would most likely have to go back to the shelter and have to change school again.

The counselor made her promise to keep her abreast of the conditions or else she would have to report it. Ruthie did not tell her everything that was going on there. Anyway, Mrs. Velez helped her to get a part-time job at one of the Fast Food chains so she would have money for food. She worked anywhere from ten to fifteen hours weekly and sometimes much more. Mrs Velez helped her open a savings account and she kept the bank book so Mrs. Brenes would not know how much she was saving. When Ruthie got her first check Mrs. Brenes asked to see it. When Ruthie walked in the house she called to her.

"Ruthie come here Honey, let me see that big check."

Ruthie walked over to her and hand it to her, as she spoke

"Oh, I don't think it is very big, but just enough to buy my dinner so you don't have to worry about saving anything for me".

"Do you want me to cash it for you?"

"Oh! no, I" ll do it myself."

"Well, anytime you need me to cash your check, just let me know."

"Thank you, I will."

The check was only for thirty dollars and Mrs Brenes knew it wasn't much to last her buying food for the next two weeks.

When Ruthie moved into the Brenes' home she was told by Mrs. Brene that her sons were in and out, but not living there permanently. She was told that the State were not aware of there goings and comings and that she would appreciate it if she did not mention it to her Counselor in any conversation they may have. Ruthie thought very little of what she had said. Ruthie liked the school and her teachers. Mrs. Brenes sons seem the be at her home all the time but they did not bother her at that time. She was in and out and did not make a habit of befriending them. When Ruthie came in the house when they were around she would go to her room and work on a school project or other homework. Most times she was tired from work and already ate. She would pay her respects to Mr. and Mrs. Brenes and the others. The other girl she shared a room with was always hanging around the family, especially the boys. She knew Marlo was always in the boys face or hanging out in their room. They were in the same school. In the beginning she tried to wait and walk to school with her but soon realized it was a waste of time, because if Mr. and Mrs. Brenes left before they went to school, Marlo did not bother to leave the house. She remained at home hanging out with the guys doing what ever. When the guys began to make passes at her, she try to ignore them and let them know she was not interested in what they tend to have in mind.

Ruthie managed to stay there a year before it became almost impossible to stay any longer. Mrs. Brenes' sons were stoned drug addicts. She kept moth balls and good toilet water around her clothing so she would not smell like she lived on a marijuana farm. The other girl her age that lived there was messing around with the oldest boy, Tom. Since she shared the room with Marlo, Ruthie knew how often Tom would find his way into the room without his mother knowing. More times than enough, she would find them in the bed and they would beg her not to tell. When they got tired of her walking in on them, Tom got his brother Bob to try making out with her.

Mrs. Brenes was at church that evening assisting with a funeral. Ruthie got home a bit later than usual. She was tired because she went directly from school to work and they were busy. She worked more hours that evening than she ever did, plus she had to walk eight blocks to get home. She was so tired, she forgot and left her food at work. When she got home she knew it was needless to look for food at the Brenes's, so she went up to her room to do her school work. She pushed open the door and there was Marlo and Tom in bed and Bob in her bed. She just stood there speechless. Bob stretched out his arms, signaling for her.

"Hey, Ruthie, baby, I have been waiting for you, come on over here and give me a kiss. Want a smoke? It is guaranteed to make you feel good and it will open up your mind to all things. Don't just stand there, come on Baby, Let's get it on."

"No, thank you, I'll wait until your mother comes, maybe she can find me another place to sleep because sex and drugs are not my thing. Sex will be when I get married and the only drugs I take will be from a licensed physician and even then, I will question him or her."

"Listen to Miss cutie." Bob got out of the bed and walked toward Ruthie.

"I said I am waiting for you baby and I want you now. I promise not to hurt you."

Ruthie starts to walk away, toward the stairs. Bob grabbed her as he spoke.

"Look tramp, you are in my house and you will do what I say." Ruthie fought back in anger as she spoke.

"You want to bet? If you don't let me go, both of us will end up at the bottom of the stairs. Now let me go."

Mrs. Carter had made sure Ruthie had lessons in self-defense shortly after she came to live with them and at that moment Bob did not know who he was dealing with and was trying to force himself on.

Another thing, Mrs Carter had told her was never brag or tell anyone all your secrets, let things come as a surprise to them at the right time.

Marlo and Tom were a bit upset because Ruthie broke up their party by not joining in.

Ruthie went back to her room, took the covers off her bed and headed out the door to the laundromat. Marlo spoke, her anger was quite apparent.

"What's the matter, trying to be cute, huh? Ruthie answered.

"Cute? just because I won't let that slob lay all over me?

No Honey, not cute. What you do is your business and what I do is mine, just don't involve me in your matters and affairs because I know what I want out of life and I hope you know what you want and where what you are doing will lead.

Marlo, look at us. Our parents don't want us, that's why we are here. (Ruthie didn't know that Marlo's parents were deceased) If you get pregnant, what will you do at age fifteen with a baby? Do you think Tom will marry you? He cannot even take care of himself. I am not putting you down, nor am I trying to hurt your feelings, but I do not want to see you hurt anymore or hurt someone else. Tell me what would you do with a child right now? You know what? If you get pregnant they will send you back to the shelter and when the child is born, put it up for adoption. Do you know what I am trying to say? Your child may end up in a place like this in a few years, if a home is not found. Marlo, get high on education and let your experience be the satisfaction. Nobody will love and care for you, but you. Do you understand what I mean?"

"Ah, it is you who do not understand, Ruthie. If we just play along with these guys, we can be assured of a place to stay. This is not a bad place to stay, I've been in worse places. If you are afraid of getting pregnant, why don't you get on the pill? "

"Because I don't feel it 's necessary. I want to remain a virgin because when I get married, nor do I want to explain to my husband who I went to bed with. I want it to be an important occasion, not a rushed thing. I am going to wash my things, be back soon."

Bob watched Ruthie as she walked down the stairs and out the door. She put up such a fight, he developed a greater determination to have her.

After that encounter, Ruthie felt a bit uneasy around Bob especially when he started acting all nice to her. She tried to stay away from the house as much as possible, when Mrs. Brene was not there.

Ruthie started attending church. She joined and was there for all meetings when she was not at school, or work. Mrs. Brene was proud of her and it made her look good with the Youth Placement Center. Ruthie gets Marlo to go to church sometimes, but not often. Marlo was to much into sex and grass.

During the Winter months, in New England, it was hard on poor people, like the Brenes. There was very little work for Mr Brene and their sons beat them out of every little extra money they had, so they really only had what they received from the State for Marlo and Ruthie.

The weather took its toll on Ruthie because she had to walk from work late evenings. She kept her job though. There were times when the weather was nice and she went to work and business was slow and she was the first to go home. She knew they did that, because she was Black. However, she continued to work.

One evening, it snowed for three hour straight. All the while she was hoping they would send her home because she had to walk (and they knew it) but, times like this she was the last to leave. She never complained, just continued to work as she always did. Some off the others started slowing down as if they were tired and getting nasty with the few customers. They wanted to be sent home. Most of them had cars or their parents would pick them up. As for Ruthie, she had to walk eight blocks and it was cold and icy. After the last customer left and it seemed like no one else was coming in, Herb, the manager, came up to her and said.

"Ruthie, after you finish cleaning that area, you can leave, I will be closing up. Will someone be picking you up? My wife called, she said it's bad out there and a dog should not be out in that weather."

"Yes, it sure looks bad out there. I usually walk home."

"I think you better call someone to pick you up. You sure cannot walk and there is no way I can take you. I will be lucky to make it home myself."

"No Herb, you don't have to worry, I'll make it."

Herb looked at her and shook his head.

Ruthie knew the weather conditions and she was prepared, but not what she had to face that night.

It was cold, the snow was blowing in her face, the streets were icy and covered with snow. Ruthie slipped and slide all the way home. She wished there was someone she could call to give her a ride. She was cold and praying to make it without falling. She was walking on the sidewalk and sometimes in the middle of the roads when no cars were coming or going. When she reached home she was exhausting. But she made it without many problems. The fear of slipping and falling was of great concern. She was in good health and was always involved in some activities, so that helped kept her and besides she was good on Ice Skates when she lived with the Carters. Ruthie thought for a moment, "I wonder what happen to my ice skates? Could they still be at the Carter's? I must asked my Caseworker the next time I talk to her." She murmured to herself as she was walking into the house.

It took her about fifteen minutes longer to get home.

Marlo, Tom, and Bob were home when she got there. Mrs. Brene had called to let them know that she and Mr. Brene were stuck at church and was unsure when they would get home. Ruthie took off her things to thaw out. The house was cold, they ran out of fuel. She started upstairs to get ready for bed. She could tell what Marlo, Tom and Bob were doing and by drinking they could not feel the cold. Marlo followed her into the room.

"Ruthie, I know you are not going to sleep alone tonight, you will freeze. I am going to get in bed with Tom. He has a small heater in his room, so why don't you come in with us? You can sleep with Bob, he would love that."

"No thanks Marlo I will be alright."

It wasn't the first time the Brenes had ran out of fuel. Ruthie purchased a small bed warmer and hid it under her mattress, in hopes that no one would find it, she had hope they would not know she had it and complain that the use of it would run up their electric bill because they were always complaining about the electric bill as well as other bills. No one noticed when she plugged it in because there was an outlet at the head of her bed.

No sooner than Marlo got back to the room and told Bob what she said, Bob came barging into the room.

"What's with you? You would rather freeze in this room than sleep with me?"

"Look Bob, you do not have to worry about me."

"I do worry because I like you a lot. Come here baby."

"Bob, please leave." Bob took Ruthie in his arms and tried to kiss her. She pushed him away.

"Bob, I ask you to leave this room right now and do not try that again."

"Who do you think you are? Since you don't want to give me what I want then I will take it.

Ruthie was cold and frightened and she knew Bob meant business. He was a tall and handsome fellow and not used to being rejected by a homeless kid who had no place to go but where she was placed because their parents could not handle them nor did they want them for various reasons. Some children refused to go to school, some got pregnant or molested by a relative, some lost their parents and had no relatives to care for them.

Bob just knew Ruthie should have long since let him have his way with her because she was a "Nobody" anyway. (Maybe a teen hooker for all he knew) He held her so tight Ruthie could barely move. Again he tried to kiss her, she jerked her face away to the other side. Just holding her and her trying to wiggle her way out excited him even more. Ruthie could have ruined him for life, but she didn't want to hurt him that way unless it was absolutely necessary.

She pleaded with him again.

"Bob, please let me go."

"No"

The more she denied him, the angrier he got and the more he wanted to show her, he was the boss. He started to rip her clothes off. She still fought him. Just when he thought he had her Ruthie lift her leg and it caught him right in the stomach. He fell to his knees and Ruthie grabbed her coat and boots and ran out the house.

She got to the Police Station about six blocks away and told them what happened. She felt bad for the Brenes, but she could not lie. When Mrs. Brenes found out she saw a side of her that she never knew existed. Mrs. Brene called her all kinds of names and accused her of lying on her son. She told her --her son would not have trash like her and she thought she was doing her a favor by taking her in.

With these statements, Ruthie was quite confused, because Mr. and Mrs. Brene were ardent church goers and she heard them confess to their loyalty in serving to "GOD"

In church, she was happy when she heard that because then she knew she would be there with them for a long time. Her only problem was to tell them about Bob or try to stay out of his way. Now, today, to hear those words coming from Mrs. Brene, she had to wonder what it really meant to go to church and serve "GOD". It seem so wrong for a person to change so quickly and in such a evil way, especially when Jesus suffered so much for us. How can a person thank GOD over and over for the many wonderful things that God helped us obtain time and time and then forget so quickly.

Ruthie felt that if she was guilty of any of those awful things said about her, she would not feel so bad, so she turned to look at Bob.

"Please, tell your mother the truth, if you remember, I told you more than once I was not into sex and drugs and that I had no intentions of trying either one. Please at least tell your parents the truth. I have never tried to entice you. I have always tried to stay out of your way."

"Look, don't expect me to clear your record. I am a man and I don't know why you tried to stop me this time. All the other times you practically raped me."

Ruthie started to cry. She was taken back to the shelter and Marlo was removed from the Brenes' home as well which upset her very much. Ruthie and Marlo were housed at the same shelter. Both of them were required to undergo a physical examination and blood test within twenty-four hours of their removal from the Brenes home.

Also their school records were to be reviewed by the Division of Youth Board, along with their medical records. All the reports had to be in within a two week period from the time of the incident which caused Ruthie and Marlo to leave the Brenes, and the time awaiting the review board. Ruthie was looked upon unfavorably because of the accusations. The Brenes had friends on the board. Marlo hated her guts, but she did thank her for not telling on her.

Marlo did everything she could to discredit anything negative Ruthie said about the Brenes, especially Tom and Bob.

When the request came to the school for a report on Ruthie and Marlo, Mrs. Velez, Ruthie's school counselor, whom she confided in, requested to be at the Review Board.

Since no criminal complaint was filed against Bob(at the request of Ruthie) he was required to be at the review board meeting to clear himself of any statements made against him and they would decide if charges would be made.

At the review board meeting, each person was questioned. The entire Brene family and the Pastor of her church, the school counselor, her employer, Herb and some of the members at the church with Ruthie who knew Bob and Tom as they really were.

One important medical record showed that Ruthie never had intercourse, her blood show no kind of drugs or alcohol in her system or ever for months prior to the test, her school records showed very good grades and no absentees In fact, she had been on the honor roll since she started that school and schools prior. Ruthie's employer had only praises for her work ethics.

The church Pastor testified of Ruthie's character as if she was not a part of the church. His main thrust was to protect the Brenes' who were long standing members. The police comment on the state which she was in when she came into the Station.

Ruthie could see the different people coming out after being questioned, but they could not see her. She was in a sad state of mind. She wondered how many more lies would be told about her and how many the Review Board would believe. When she saw Marlo go in she hoped she would at least, tell the truth about her. She kept her secret, why couldn't she be honest about her. Marlo walked in and sat down. The director spoke first.

"Marlo Keen, I don't want you to be frightened, I just want you to tell the truth. You can make it easier on Ruthie, the Brenes and yourself. We have your medical records as well as Ruthie's and these records show someone is lying. Now, since you were there, I want you to tell me who?"

"I don't know anything. The house was cold and Tom and Bob had a heater in their room, so I went in to warm up before going to bed. If Ruthie told you anything different, she is lying."

The Board already knew Marlo was a pathological liar and it was almost useless to question her, however, they had hoped for the best. Marlo's medical records proved her to be active sexually and other tests showed an extreme amount of drugs in her system. She was also absent from school a lot and the times she was there, she cut half of her classes. When the questioning got to Mrs. Brene, it was found that she was unaware of ninety-five percent of what was going on in her house and Mr. Brene was no better off.

Mrs. Velez, the counselor from the school, was the mother of four children (two boys and two girls) She knew Mr. and Mrs. Carter younger sister and a few other relatives and they had alerted her concerning Ruthie because they saw her potential. When they both died within two weeks of each other, she was quite upset and concerned about Ruthie, but there was very little she could do. She had four children of her own and just no room for another. Some of the Carters relatives tried following Ruthie's activities, but none wanted the responsibilities of rearing a child. They knew about all Mr. and Mrs. Carter had planned for Ruthie.

She told the board what a good student Ruthie was and that she had come to her with some concerns. They were not supposed to know about the bank account and her savings, so she kept that between the two of them. They both felt that when Ruthie became of age she would have something to start out with. Since Ruthie did not tell her all that was going on in the home she could not speak on that. She told them that she was a very pleasant and humble young lady, a good student, never missed classes, did her school work as well as helped others. she told the board.

"There is nothing negative I can say about her."

When Ruthie was questioned every one was in the room. When she first spoke.

"Mrs. Velez, I must say, you are most kind. You were always there when I needed you. I will take that back. You were there most times when I needed you." Her eyes went toward Mrs. Brene, I am sorry if you folks got in trouble because of me. I tried to tell Bob, that when i have sex it is going to be with my husband and another thing, I could not have laid around your house with your son. Just because I do not have parents who care about me, that is no reason to be a tramp. I am not that kind of person. I respect you and your home. I have always looked upon you as a good christian lady and from what I read in the Bible Christ did not change as fast as you turned on me. Falsely accusing me of things I could never do if Christianity does that to you, I want no part of it. Pastor Rawley, take my name off your church list because I do not want to be like you people. I want to be like the Christ I read about in the bible. I want to serve with people that are honest, good, kind, loving and understanding to everyone. I want to do things right. I don't want to lie too or on people nor do wrong things which hurt others. I want Mrs Laster, Mrs Turner, Karen and Josephine to know that I believe you are more of the kind of people that's living close to GOD. Marlo, I want you to know, even though you hate me, I still love you and I am concerned about you. My only hope is that you told the truth, if you did, that is all I can ask for, but if you did not tell the truth the GOD I know is going to get you. With that Ruthie said no more.

Mrs. Laster, Mrs. Turner, Karen, and Josephine were members of the church who worked with Ruthie in the church. Mrs. Laster was the choir director and welcomed Ruthie when she became a member of the church. She saw her potential as a leader and pushed her along. She encouraged her to become a leader and director of the Youth Choir. She showed her the "ropes" the hows, and why". Ruthie was a easy learner and caught on fast. The youth loved her and fell right in with all the developments she created. They became one of the better Youth Choirs in the areas. Ruthie learned fast. She helped to teach in the Sunday School Youth classes and was in demand on other church projects. No one show any signs of jealousy because they were happy to have the help. She became an item in the church. Ruthie was a true member and all that she did made the church and the Pastor looked good in the community. Karen and Josephine were the Pastors daughters and the looks on their face when their father had not stood up for Ruthie. They wanted to say something but the Court failed to recognize them. They looked at their father with discuss.

Karen and Josephine knew a lot more about the Brenes than their father did. They knew they were "weed" heads and always after girls. In the beginning when Ruthie started coming to their church they had to size her up (so to speak) and wonder what kind of girl she was living with the Brenes. When talking to her they knew she was different than Marlo. She never swelled like "weed". They went to the same school as Ruthie. They were happy when she appeared in church one Sunday and encouraged her to join. They started a program to help school age student to get better grade. Ruthie was there to help when she was not at work. In the time she was there, at the church several programs were developed to help in the community. Ruthie never attached her name to any of them because she told them that she was unsure how long she would be around. The credit always went to someone else in the church.

CHAPTER 2

R uthie was a very attractive girl, but she never allowed her looks to hamper her friendship with anyone much less attractive than she was.. She liked people and life had taught her to cherish love even if it is others being loved. She wanted so much to be loved by others. She always carried herself as if she could deal with any problem or issue.

Ruthie was sixteen now and a well endowed young lady. She kept up her grades in the worst schools and was hard to place in another home because of her age and good looks. Most women feared her good looks. Ruthie wanted to be placed so she could get a job. While in the shelter they were not allowed to work outside. She wanted to go to college in order to be better prepared for life and a good husband, when she got married. Ruthie knew she had only two years in the Youth Care Program. She would need a place to stay when she was released and that cost money.

After about six months, a foster home was found. A Mr. and Mrs. Crossley. Ruthie did not care for the Mister, but they were her only hope, so far. Mrs. Crossley asked her a lot of questions and even wanted to know if she was on the pill. When Ruthie said "no" , she was alarmed. Ruthie assured her if she ever felt she needed them (pills), she would let her know. Life with Crossleys was not bad, nor was it exceptably good. She was allowed to work certain hours and in the beginning, she had to give a portion of her money to the Crossleys, for safe- keeping, they said. Well, anyway, they made her give only ten dollars out of each check. She earned forty dollars weekly, sometimes more or less. She was careful the way she spent her money. When the Crossleys realized why she wanted to work and how considerate she was, they told her to keep the ten dollars and add it to her savings account, but if they had to pick her up from work she would have to pay them.

Ruthie expressed her appreciation and promise that she would not let them down.

Mrs. Crossley was another church goer, but not as hypocritical as the Brenes. Ruthie would accompany her many times just to have some place to go and also so she would not be left alone with Mr. Crossley. She did not like the way he watched her, it reminded her of the way Bob Brene looked at her. Mrs. Crossley had her eyes on him as well. She was always glad when Ruthie offered to come with her. She was in the habit of expecting her to follow her. Many times when she had to work on Sundays, Mrs. Crossley would be waiting for her when she came in from work.

Ruthie came in from school one day to find Mrs. Crossley in great pain. She contacted her doctor and left a message for Mr Crossley, at work to let him know that the doctor said for her to take her to the hospital right away.

"Mrs. Crossley, the doctor said for you to go to the hospital right now, he will meet you there."

"No, tell him to call in a prescription for pain, I'll be alright."

"The doctor said for you to come right away. I already called a taxi.". It did not take much for her to figure out, even with as much pain as she was in, why she did not want to leave.

"Mrs, Crossley, I will run upstairs and pack a few things because I don't think I will be allowed to stay here if you are not here. I will get you settled and explain to the shelter if they keep you in the hospital, okay?"

Ruthie was up and down the stairs with her bag in five minutes. The taxi came and took them to the hospital and Ruthie stayed right by Mrs

Crossley's side during the examination. It was her "gall bladder" This was a problem she had been trying to avoid for sometime.

They were getting her ready for surgery when Mr. Crossley arrived. Ruthie filled him in while they waited for the doctor to come out. After he talked to the doctor and they took Mrs. Crossley to surgery, Mr, Crossley decided to go home to shower and change clothing.

"Ruthie, you can come home with me. I must get washed up. Mrs. Crossley will be there for a while. You can come back with me, if you like."

"No, that's alright, I will be okay." Ruthie got in touch with her caseworker and explained what happened and that she would prefer to stay at the shelter until Mrs. Crossley got out of the hospital. She explained that she would be staying at the hospital until Mrs. Crossley was out of surgery, then she would take the bus in. Everything was alright with them and she was told to call when Mrs. Crossley got out of surgery."

When Mrs. Crossley was fully awakened Ruthie got ready to leave, it was four o'clock in the morning. Ruthie phoned the shelter.

"Hello, Mrs Kohn, this is Ruthie. Mrs. Crossley is going to be alright and since it is so early in the morning I will go to school and work and report in after I get done work, if it's okay with you? I have been napping off and on all night and I am alright."

Mrs Kohn knew Ruthie was one person who could be trusted. Ruthie left her bags in Mrs. Crossley's room, after getting approval from the nurse on duty.

After school she had to work three hours. When she finished work, she went by the house to pick up a few things, take a shower, change clothes and get to the hospital to pick up her bag. On the way out the door, Mr. Crossley came up.

"Where are you going?" all the while, he was holding her hand. He pulled her over to him.

I want to thank you for what you did, taking my wife to the hospital and calling me and all"

He kissed her cheek. Ruthie pulled away.

"That's alright Mr, Crossley, you and Mrs. Crossley are my parents right now. I bet you were one of the best fathers to your children."

"Well, I did the best I Could, thanks."

"I better go, they are waiting for me at the shelter. I am not allowed to live here until Mrs Crossley returns. I will be going to the hospital after school or after work, whichever."

Ruthie left before he could say another word. She took the bus to the hospital, visited with Mrs. Crossley for a while and headed for the shelter. She knew she would only be there for a few days because that would be about the length of time Mrs. Crossley was expected to be hospitalized. For this once, she received special privilege to remain at the shelter and keep her job, if she paid her transportation expenses when necessary. She was required to be in before 10: PM. That was fine with Ruthie because she wanted more than anything to keep her job.

When Ruthie did not have to work, she would spend more time at the hospital with Mrs. Crossley, helping her walk around. She got to know many of the nurses and they liked her very much. She would volunteer to run errands for them when Mrs. Crossley was busy with treatments or visitors. Mrs. Crossley got extra special care because of Ruthie.

Being around the hospital that length of time made Ruthie quite interested in becoming a nurse.

Mrs. Connors was the Head Nurse on duty when Ruthie came around and she would always go into Mrs. Crossley's room. Mrs. Crossley would always give Ruthie the (Third degree) when she came in.

"Were you by the house and did you see Mr. Crossley today?"

"No, I was only there that one time I told you about and I have not seen Mr. Crossley since. Is there something you want me to do?"

It was always the same questions. There were times when Ruthie thought about not going to visit, but she went anyway. One day while Ruthie was sitting in the cafeteria eating a snack, Mrs. Connors came in and joined her because she wanted to ask a few personal questions.

"Ruthie, may I join you?"

"Sure."

"I have been watching you. I believe you would make an excellent nurse. Have you thought about becoming one?"

"Yes, more and more each day I come around here."

"How are your grades at school?"

"I've been on the honor roll for the past five years and if I wasn't Black with an unstable home I would be more visitable."

"Why do you say that, do you know that you should be? "

"Yes, my work is better than many of the honor students. Many times I help them with their work. They even offer to pay me for answers, but I don't want their money, I help for nothing."

"Why does Mrs. Crossley ask you all those questions about Mr. Crossley? "

"I don't know."

"I bet you do know but do not want to talk about it."

"Maybe I think I know, but I'm not sure. It's like I don't really know."

"Will you stay with them after you turn eighteen?"

"No!"

"Where will you go?"

"I hope to have enough money saved to get my own place and go to college. I have been working and saving since I was fifteen. Right now I need a much better job---part time for now with the possibility of becoming full time after I finish school. Mrs. Connors, I want so much to have a place I can call home. That means so very much to me."

"I can understand that. Have you decided what you will do in college?"

"I am thinking very strongly about nursing."

"When you decide, let me know."

"I will be graduating High School next year."

"Look, I will talk to my husband. He is a Physician and if he gets an opening in his office, he will hire you, I am sure. The pay would be much better than what you are receiving now. Just maybe he will give you a few more hours. Also during the summer you can work full time."

Ruthie went on to explain the accusations made by her parents and others and the incident at the Brenes. They exchanged addresses and Ruthie gave Mrs Connors the name of her Caseworker and her father. She did not want to hide anything about herself which may come up later. She talked about the Carters and how they were trying to adopt her. Mrs. Connors had a good idea of the type of person Ruthie was because of her honesty. She did not feel Ruthie was trying to hide anything from her nor play on her sympathy.

In less than two weeks Mr, Crossley was out of the hospital. Ruthie came back to live with them the following day. She was back into her routine of going to school and working as well and doing most of the work around the house. Mrs. Crossley was always a good housekeeper, so her house was not dirty, only dusty. When Ruthie did not have to work, she offered her assistance. She cooked, cleaned and ran errands. The type of surgery Mrs. Crossley had and the complication after it took her a while to get back into the swing of things.

After Mrs. Crossley was home about a week, she developed some additional problems and had to be bedridden. The doctor kept her on medication which made her drowsy because she was in quite a bit of pain. It was not necessary for her to be hospitalized, however, at home, they had to keep a close watch on her just in case she got worse, then she would have to be admitted back into the hospital.

The Crossley children were scattered and they had their own families to care for, so they could not be there as often as necessary to help. Most of the time, Ruthie and Mr. Crossley had to watch over her and take care of her needs. Mrs. Crossley had reached a state where she refused to take the medications and one night, because she was in so much pain, the doctor had to come out and give her a shot, which really put her to sleep. Ruthie was glad because she was tired. She was always the person who catered to Mrs. Crossley's needs at night because Mr. Crossley worked and he would go right off to sleep in the other bedroom. This particular night, when Mr. Crossley was assured that his wife was knocked out, he got into Ruthie's bed, after the doctor left. When Ruthie walked into her room she was startled.

"Come on and lay down with me, I know you are tired. I just want to hug and kiss you because you have been such a big help to me. Come on, don't be afraid, you are such a beautiful young lady. How many boyfriends have you had?"

"None Sir, and I don't think it would be right for you and I to be in the same bed together, I am sure that Mrs. Crossley wouldn't like that."

Ruthie was so afraid, she had hope that she would not have to go through the same thing she went through with Bob Brene. Tears began to well up in her eyes. Through her tears, she began to blurt out to Mr. Crossley what had happened to her at the Brene's and as a result, what she had done to prevent anything from coming of it. Mr. Crossley was a bit frightened and he apologized.

"I am sorry, I would not have tried or done anything like that. I am a father to you now. I will not say the same when you are older. Please don't think I meant anything other than a fatherly hug and kiss. Oh! I guess you want to get in your bed. I am so tired, I got into the first bed I saw."

Just about now, Mr. Crossley was up and on his way out the door. He looked back at a frightened little girl.

"Forgive me, I did not mean any harm. Good night."

Through her tears, which were just about gone, Ruthie spoke.

"Good night Sir."

After that night, Ruthie never trusted him and she stayed out of his way as much as possible. Mrs. Crossley was bedridden for almost two weeks, after a few more weeks, she was her old self again.

Ruthie had gotten to know a lot of the young people at church and would go on outings with them. This kept her away from the house a lot.

Mrs. Crossley had it in her mind that Ruthie and her husband were messing around when she was ill. She looked for an opportunity to find out anything she could. Ruthie had gained a little weight over the winter and in Mrs. Crossley's mind, she told herself Ruthie was pregnant.

She got her chance to have her examined the day she came home, after a church dinner with an upset stomach.

Ruthie walked in the door with tears in her eyes.

"Mrs. Crossley, I feel sick, my stomach hurts real bad."

She just made it to the bathroom. Mrs. Crossley waited until she thought she was alright.

"How do you feel now?"

"Much better, it must have been the salad, I thought it tasted kind of funny."

"Just to make sure, I am taking you to the doctor."

"I feel alright now."

"That's fine, but I want to be sure. No ifs, and or buts now, I know you took such good care of me when I was ill, so let's go young lady."

Ruthie didn't argue. When they got to the doctor's office, Mrs. Crossley went in and spoke to him first.

In his examination, the doctor pressed all over Ruthie's stomach.

"Does that hurt?"

"No, not hurt, but it is a little sore."

"I want you to take off everything and put on this gown. I might as well give you a good physical because Mrs. Crossley will give me a hard time if you go home and get sick again".

When the doctor completed the physical, Ruthie got dressed. The doctor went out to talk to Mrs. Crossley.

"Your girl is alright. It probably was something she ate. I'll give you a prescription for her stomach, if she has any more problems call me."

"Oh! Doctor, you are sure she is not pregnant?"

"Mrs. Crossley, I am very sure, because she has never been with a man and you cannot be any more surer than that."

"Thanks Doctor, that took a lot off my shoulders."

Ruthie came out of the room and the doctor discussed the medication with her. Mrs. Crossley was a lot less hostile and they were able to talk.

CHAPTER 3

••••••••••••••••••••••••••••••••

Mrs. Conners, the lady from the hospital, finally called to see if Ruthie could go talk to her husband about the job.

"Ruthie, how have you been?"

"Fine, how are things at the hospital?"

"Okay, I just called to see if you are still interested in that job in my husband's office?"

"I sure am."

"Well, when can I set up an appointment for you?"

"Any time after school or before five o'clock."

"What time do you get out of school?"

"At two o'clock."

"Okay, what about tomorrow at three?"

"That sounds alright to me."

"Are you sure Mrs. Crossley won't need you for anything?"

"Yes, I always talk to her about my weekly activities so I will know what hours I can work anyway, and it's very rare that she intervenes with my plans."

"Good! You know where his office is located?"

"Yes, and thanks a lot."

"Give me a call afterward and tell me what you decide."

"I sure will, I just feel like I got the job already."

When Ruthie hung up the phone, she was elated. She thought Mrs. Connor had forgotten about her, she tried to call her several times but she was either out or quite busy at work.

The following day Ruthie went for the interview. She spoke with the nurse at the office and then to Doctor Connors. They seemed quite pleased with her responses. The doctor thanked her for coming in.

"Miss Warren, I want to thank you for coming in and I will let you know my decision in a few days."

"Thank you Doctor Connors, I will look forward to your decision."

Ruthie was a little disappointed. She had thought the doctor would let her know right away if he was going to hire her. She left there and went to work at the Fast Food job. After work she went right home.

Ruthie did not allow herself to get involved with boyfriends because of the way she was forced to live (A ward of the State) living in various foster homes or a shelter when no home wanted to be bothered with you. For all she knew she was labeled incorrigible and a victim of an unwanted pregnancy, even though her parents were married and had other children. (She, they did not want) She still could not understand, why? She was never a bad child. Her Sisters and brothers were much worse than she. Her mother showed some love to her but her father rarely touched her or spoke to her. He treated her as if he wanted nothing to do with her. How could she explain that to a teenage boy when she did not understand herself? The times she did talk to boys they thought she was easy because she was a ward of the state and should do whatever they wanted, but, when they found her different, they did not know how to handle her. She found it hard to believe but girls felt the same way about her. They even believed that she had a couple of pregnancies. Ruthie ran into so much of this kind of flack, so much so that she decided to stay to herself and use her time to study and work. She found at an early age that she could solve a problem in trigonometry faster than she could make others realize she was a normal healthy human being, wanting friendship with people her own age. Ruthies's best friend was the "Library" and a detail study of some project she selected, such as History or Science.

Life with the Crossleys was difficult at times because of the little indications from Mr. Crossley and the suspiciousness of Mrs Crossley. Mrs. Crossley would watch her constantly and never allow her in the house alone with Mr. Crossley. If Ruthie was out of school and did not have to work. She had to leave the house when she did. Ruthie would follow her around when she could or utilize her time in the library, reading or researching a paper for school just to get extra credit. She had so few friends because of what they were doing. Even though they did not care to hang around her she felt the same way about them.

Doctor Connors called Ruthie about a week later to let her know she got the job and to see if she could start work the following week. The very next day Ruthie typed up a letter of resignation to give to her boss. She wanted to resign in a diplomatic way. So that if she should return or ever need references she would not have a problem. Her letter read.

Dear Mr. Bushnick:

I wish to thank you for hiring me and allowing me to remain on the job for the period of fourteen months.

I hope that my leaving will not put you in a bind but I must move onto a better paying job and more hours. I will soon be on my own and paying rent as well as being totally responsible for myself.

My last day of work will be May 16.

Thank you again,

Ruthie L Warren

When the manager read the letter, he was quite impressed. On her last day of work, he gave her a twenty five dollar gift certificate.

On Ruthie's new job she was paid two dollars more than the last job, she also received ten more hours than the last job. One of the things her new job had was a savings plan which would come out of the check before she saw it. This fit right into her plan because she did not have to worry about anyone finding her bank book. The Crossleys never question how much she earned or the hours she worked because Mrs. Crossley did not want her around the house anyway. They still only thought she was working a few hours at the new job. The time Mrs. Crossley was with her when she cashed a check for forty dollars, she thought that was what she earned every week. Since Ruthie was not a clothes freak, she was able to save, not that she didn't dress well, she kept the few clothes she had in good shape.

Ruthie continued to work for Dr. Connors and she continued to develop more beautifully,

As she grew older Mrs. Crossley continued to become more jealous. She needed the money she received for her care and she knew she would be leaving when she reached eighteen, so she did her best to allow her to stay.

However, as Ruthie came closer to her eighteenth birthday things were becoming more unbearable and she knew it was best to start looking for a place to live. Ruthie came in from work one day, really feeling bad, she had a fever of a hundred and three. The Doctor gave her an antibiotic to take and told her to stay in bed a couple days. Since it was Friday, it proposed a problem, but she felt too bad to think about it. When she got home Mrs. Crossley was there.

"Hello, Mrs. Crossley."

"What are you doing at home? Didn't you have to work?"

"Yes, but the doctor sent me home. I have a fever. He told me to stay in bed for a few days. Please call him, he will explain."

"If you are so sick, why didn't they put you in the hospital? We don't need you spreading any germs around here."

"He said, it's just a virus, nothing to worry about."

"If it's nothing to worry about, why did he send you home?"

"I feel lousy, do you mind if I try to eat this soup and go to bed?, I will stay in my room and only come out when I have to."

"Make sure you do just that. I may need you to do some shopping for me if I have to go away tomorrow."

Ruthie thought, (what will I do and where will I go if this lady makes me leave when she goes tomorrow. I wish she would stop yapping and let me eat so I can take this medicine and go to bed. God, I hope this medicine gets me well enough to go to school and work Monday. If it was hot enough I could go to the beach, but it's cold out. Three more months before graduation and in four months, I will be eighteen, then I can leave here) Ruthie went into the kitchen, opened a can of soup, heated it and ate about half of it. Mrs. Crossley was still trying to hold a questioning conversation. She never ceases to ask one more question.

"Ruthie, have you thought about where you will be living? You know you have four more months here?"

"I know, I am not sure if I will be living around here. I will be going to college as soon as I find out which one I will be attending. I will be looking for a place close by."

"Where do you think you are going to get the money for college?"

"I have been applying for scholarships and I am sure I can get a student loan."

"You cannot use that money for an apartment."

"I have been saving most of my money I earned, that will help."

"My dear the little money you earned, will not sustain you for very long. Do you know the cost of renting an apartment these days?"

"Yes, I have been checking. Would you like some of this soup?"

"No, thank you."

"Well, I am going to leave it here and try eating it later. I am going to take this medicine now and lie down. I am going to take this juice to the room, if you don't mind. Can I do anything for you before I lay down?"

"No, Just lock your door, so no one will disturb you."

Ruthie slept for about two hours and was awakened by a loud rap on her door. She got up to open the door. It was Mrs. Leys, her caseworker and Mrs. Crossley.

"Hi, Mrs Leys, I hope you didn't have to wait very long. I have a virus, the doctor said and I do feel lousy, come on in. Is something wrong? You are out on a Friday night?"

"No, I just want to check on you. Let me see your medication, Oh! It's a prescription?"

"Yes, the doctor never gives me samples. He said it is more ethical since I have to live this way. He doesn't want anyone questioning any medication he prescribes for me."

"How did you get so sick? Did you catch something from his patients?"

"No! I think I think from school because a lot of kids were out this week. I was hoping it didn't get a hold of me, but, I guess it did."

"Is that your only problem?"

"What do you mean?"

"You are not messing around out there are you?"

"No, indeed, It is only the virus, that is all."

"Mrs. Crossley tells me you are planning to go to college."

"Yes, I am, and if you know of any grants or scholarships which I haven't applied for, please let me know." She went over fumbling through her books and returned with a typewritten paper of the name and places and dates where and when she applied for different grants and scholarships. She handed it to her caseworker.

"Here is my list of the places I applied for tuition aid. I will get a copy made for you and bring it by next week. I don't want to give you that one because it is the only one I have and anyway, I have a few more to add to the list." Mrs. Leys took the paper and was amazed.

"I must say I do believe you want to go to college. I understand your grades are very good at school. You may get a few from your school. What do you plan to major in?"

"I really would like to become a Doctor, "

"A Doctor? You must be joking! Do you realize the number of years you must attend college and the cost?"

"Well, I guess, but I was also thinking about working-maybe I will settle for nursing first."

"That is a good area to think about and the money is not bad either."

"" It is not so much the money I am concerned with, it's just that I like helping people who really need it."

"What about social work? That's a necessary field and we help a lot of people. We helped you."

"Mrs. Leys, I was not the one with the real problem. It is true that my parents did not want me, but the reasoning behind it I don't quite understand and I don't think they did either. They took care of my other sisters and brothers. Why not me? Somehow, I feel they should have had a lot more counseling than me. One day I am going to find out what went wrong that caused my parents to turn against me. Although you folks tried to help me, do you realize all the problems I faced in the process."

"Are you having problems here?" Ruthie did not answer that question directly. She said, "In four months, I will be leaving and plan to be packed the night before I turn eighteen."

"What is wrong? Mrs. Crossley speaks very highly of you."

"Mrs. Leys, I go to school and I get good grades because I utilize my time wisely. I go to church, never give them any trouble and I don't mess around with boys, nor wild crowds. Mr. Leys, I try real hard not to hurt anyone or cause problems in any way, but I am still not trusted, nor do I feel comfortable here. I am trying real hard not to have to go anywhere else until I can get my own place. I would like you, if you have time, to give me some pointers on how to make it on my own. I am learning a lot in school, but the more knowledge I have, the more selection I'll have to choose from. Would you mind if I call you with questions even if I am no longer in your care?"

"Please do, I will do whatever I can to help you. Would you like to go into a halfway house for a few months, if you cannot afford an apartment when you leave here?"

"What would that be like?"

"You would live with other girls who are living partially on their own with minimum supervision. You would work, pay your keep and learn how to manage money, things of that sort."

"I don't know, what about my plans for college?"

"You can still do the same things you plan."

"Will I have to share a room?"

"Probably, most likely. Sometimes girls can learn from one another."

"No! I think I want to be on my own. Thanks anyway," Ruthie got up and started in the kitchen. As Mrs. Leys followed.

"I think I will eat the rest of my soup and take the medicine and lay back down. I still feel a bit woozy but I think my fever has gone down. She excused herself, "I must get dressed."

Mrs. Leys said "Why don't you put a housecoat on, if you are going right back to bed."

"I am not allowed to go in any other part of the house if I am not fully dress." (Mrs. Leys eyes were beginning to open)

Ruthie was allowed to stay in that day because Mr. Crossley had to work and Mrs. Crossley stayed home from church. So Ruthie really had the chance to stay in and take her medication as the doctor ordered. By that Sunday afternoon she felt much better.

Ruthie often thought about Mr. and Mrs. Carter because it was the first real home she had. She would always go to the cemetery and put flowers on their graves on special holidays. She would go by the house to see if it was occupied, at least twice a year.

At least twice a year she would get a letter from a lawyer with a few questions she had to answer and return it in a prepaid envelope. She did not know why she just completed it and sent it back. She never questioned it nor mentioned it to anyone. She merely thought it was part of the system she was in. She even wrote them to ask if they knew of any scholarships they were aware of that she might apply for. They wanted to know her grades in school, so she would send a copy. The lawyer wanted to know if she was working, where? Did she like where she lived? why? why not? Where will she be living when she finishes high school?

This time when the letter came she was given an appointment to come into the office the day after her birthday. Ruthie thought very little about the importance of the appointment, she felt that it was only to legally release her from the state's responsibilities for her care.

Ruthie was counting the days she had left with the Crossleys. Mr. Crossley tried to get in her room several times when Mrs. Crossley stepped out for short periods. One time, Ruthie did not latch her door because she was getting ready to undress, in walked Mr. Crossley.

"Hi there, beautiful, can we talk? Come here and put your arms around me. We will be losing you soon, but if you are nice to me, I will let you stay. Come on and give me a kiss, for now."

"Mr. Crossley, what are you saying? I have always respected you and Mrs. Crossley as my parents. I don't understand. You are sounding like you are making a pass at me, someone younger than your childrens. But I know that is not what you are doing. Is this how fathers act toward their daughters? I was talking to Reverend Conglin the other day about actions such as this by men and he said it is wrong, So, Mr. Crossley, if you are making a pass, please leave my room and only come in along with Mrs. Crossley. I will explain to her why, Thank you, Sir, "

Mr. Crossley was startled by Ruthie's abruptness, also a little shaken. He wondered if Ruthie mentioned his name to the Reverend.

Mr. Crossley was thinking in terms of the types of children coming from broken homes and/is labeled as incorrigible, tending to be somewhat backward and might do anything to and for anyone. But Ruthie seemed different yet he had to try. She was such a lovely girl and desirable.

Yet he did not want his "good name" ruin, So he apologized and tried to clarify what he just indicated.

"Oh, Ruthie, I meant no disrespect. It's just that we will miss you and if you don't have a place to stay, I will discuss it with Mrs. Crossley and maybe we can work something out for you to stay here and rent you the room until you can get what you want." Grinning sheepishly, he went on. "We will not see you out in the streets without any place to go. Please don't think I was trying to be fresh. I know you are a nice girl."

He left the room quickly with his head down, deep in thought, wondering if Ruthie mentioned his name or told anyone all the times he tried to hold her in his arms.

Ruthie thought, maybe she was wrong, maybe he was only trying to be fatherly because she had seen him hug his children many times, but still, he always did things like that to her when Mrs. Crossley wasn't around. Well, she thought, regardless of whatever his reasoning behind it, she hoped he would not try that ever again or she would most surely put him in his place. She did not want to cause any problems between him and his wife when she had so little time to be there. She will make sure she is a lot more careful and alert here after.

Despite the problems in Ruthie's childhood, she graduated High School with Honors. The Crossley's were there and her caseworker Mrs. Leys. Ruthie had hoped her father and sisters and brothers would be there. She had notified them far in advance, yet still, they did not come nor acknowledge her request.

She received a thousand dollar scholarship and a few other citations recognizing her for her accomplishment. That along with the money she saved, a job, and some penny pinching would get her through two years of college without having to borrow money.

Her main problem was she needed a permanent address. Many things ran through her mind. She wishes she could rent a room until college begins and she could make college her home. Then what would happen when college closes between semesters? (It would save her money)

Everything seemed to go right back to a permanent address. She knew there was no way she could get through college without borrowing money. However, that would be her last resort. She wanted to keep her job, but where she planned on going to college was too far away. She would need a car if she was to keep her job. Well, Ruthie figured out what she was going to do. She found out that she qualified for tuition. She did not have to pay for college because of the life she had to live and that was a savings. She could easily complete and, A SOCIAL DEGREE at very little cost, afford an apartment and survive for two years with the money she had saved. Just maybe she could squeeze a car if she is careful with her money.

Working for Dr. Connor's and getting into the Nursing Program at the college would help her toward reaching her goals, if she was going to do anything with her life. She felt that she wanted to be able to have a better life so she planned to do everything in her power to achieve her goals.

Ruthie found an efficiency apartment which cost seven hundred and fifty monthly with all utilities included. The neighborhood left a lot to be desired, but she hadn't much choice.

The Youth Service will be giving her enough money for three months' care to help her get started and that would help a lot.

CHAPTER 4

The day of her birthday, Ruthie gathered all her things and moved out, but before she left, she thanked the Crossley's for allowing her to live with them the length of time they did. She gave them a gift certificate to one of the best restaurants in town which would enable them to dine at least three times. She knew they liked to eat out. On their first night out they would be receiving a dozen roses, the second time a corsage. Well, anyway, Mrs. Crossley would receive the corsage and Mr. Crossley a flower in his lapel and the third night flowers again.

The whole shabang cost Ruthie almost two hundred dollars. The Crossleys did not know what it cost Ruthie because of the way she had it set up.

The only gifts Ruthie received for her graduation and birthday were from Dr. and Mr. Connors and the others where she worked. They all gave her money and a cake on both occasions. They felt she needed the money more than gifts she may never use.

When she got all set to move out, Mr. Crossley tried to slip a twenty dollar bill into her hand.

"Oh! No! Sir, I could not take that unless it was coming from the both of you. Please don't feel that you have to do things for me behind your wife's back." She pushed the money back into his hand.

"I'll be alright, thanks anyway." Ruthie said goodbye and left. They did not bother to ask where she was going, not that she wanted them to, especially Mr. Crossley.

The apartment had a stove and a refrigerator so the only things she had to purchase was a bed, chairs for the living room area and a table for eating. Also dishes, curtains, linen and few other things. It was not expensive furniture, but it was new and she had earned the money for it. Ruthie was proud of her accomplishments and she felt at ease. She thought, "At last, my own place." She was too tired to cook that night, so she went out and picked something up from the fast food restaurant. She slept well that night.

Ruthie had an appointment with the lawyer, so she was up bright and early. She wanted to Several all ties with whatever he wanted her for. She had a light breakfast because she had no time to do any real food shopping anyway. She got to the lawyer's office about a half hour before her appointment. Since he was not busy he took her right in.

"Good morning, Miss Warren. Do you know why you are here and why I have been corresponding with you over the years?"

"No, Sir, not really. I just thought it had something to do with the State and keeping abreast of my activities until it was time to release them from all responsibilities of me. Isn't that the reason?"

"No, my dear. I was the Attorney for Mr. and Mrs. Carters."

"Sir, I will never forget them. They were the best parents anyone could ever have. I always sneak away wherever I was living and go to the cemetery and put flowers on their graves a few times a year and go by the house just to remember the good times we had together. I miss them so much. Now that I am eighteen, I wish they were here so I could do some nice things for them. Every time I think about doing something out of the ordinary, I think about all the things they taught me, then I realize they would not be pleased, so right away my thoughts change." Tears began to trickle down Ruthie's cheeks. As she spoke.

"I wonder why they had to die and leave me alone. GOD must have known I needed them so much." The lawyer spoke up.

"I believe GOD knew you could take care of yourself. Anyway, the Carters did leave something to help you on your way, in their will. They left you a sum of money which amounted to seven five thousand dollars, at the time. I took the liberty of investing it for you over the years and because of that, I am able to give you a check for one hundred thousand dollars. You are a very fortunate young lady. I knew the Carters very well and I know they were quite fond of you. Their family was very pleased with the love you brought in their home as well."

Ruthie was in a state of shock. She could not figure out the right words to say to express her gratitude, so she just listened as the lawyer continued.

"They had also discussed property for you, but had not gotten around to changing their Will, so there was nothing I could do about that. The property went to the next of kin, however, I discussed their wishes with them. It was my word against what was written in the Will and signed by them."

The lawyer encouraged Ruthie to go to the house and talk to Mrs Carter's Niece because Mrs Carter sister want to talk to her. She knew I would be seeing you when you turn eighteen.

Ruthie managed to thank the lawyer, through many tears.

She thanked the lawyer, after she calmed down and left the lawyer's office she took the check and went directly to the bank. She deposited all but two thousand dollars in her savings account. The two thousand she opened up a checking account. Ruthie went to the florist and bought a plant. She took the bus out to the cemetery where the Carters were buried and set the plant between the two graves.

The Doctor had given her a few days off to get her apartment together, so since the delivery people had bought all her furniture at the same time and she was there to show them where she wanted everything, ninety-five percent of her problems were solved.

Ruthie decided that since all this had been done, she would take the bus and visit her father who had remarried. She didn't take any clothes because she did not want them to think she wanted to stay. She made sure she would be able to get a return bus that evening. Her father lived about two hour away. She plans to stay about an hour and return home a little before dark.

Ruthie arrived at her father's house a little after two that afternoon and was met at the door by Gloria, his wife.

"Hello! I just came by to visit for a little while."

Gloria looked past her to see if she had brought any luggage.

"How long do you plan to stay?"

"Only about an hour. I want to get back home before it's too late."

"Where are you staying?"

"I am still outside of Philadelphia, but I have my own apartment now."

"Are you living with someone?"

"No, I live alone."

By this time, her father had come in and they were in the living room sitting down. He asked.

"Are you working?"

"Yes, I still work for Doctor Connors, but I will be going to college in the Fall, so I will have to find another job and maybe another place to stay."

"Well, I guess you came to us for money?"

"No, I am alright, I got a few scholarships because I was an honor student, plus I worked and saved most of my money. I have enough to live on until I finish college, whether I keep my job or not."

"You must have done a lot of saving."

"Oh yes, I make a good salary working for the Doctor because, during the Summer and holidays I usually worked full time. I allowed them to keep most of my paycheck in a savings account. All but forty dollars every week and when I had no need for that, I put that in another savings account. I did that because every little bit helps to make a difference. I never went anywhere, but to church and the movies every now and then. So I never needed a lot of clothes

"Do you have a boyfriend?"

"No, I didn't need that kind of hassle." When I was not working I was doing extra studying and it paid off. Well I just stopped by to say hello since I didn't see you folks at the graduation. Dad, you could give my sisters and brothers my address and I would like theirs because I

41

would like to drop by sometime to visit with them. Here is my address and telephone number. That incident at the Brenes, how much of it could have been Ruthie's fault?

Ruthie wanted to know about her sisters and brothers. Well, what she didn't know is that Lana had three children and was still unmarried. Eve had one and she and her husband are both alcoholics. Mike is on drugs and Eddie is in jail. Paula dropped out of school and still lives at home. Also Gloria and her three lives at home and the two cannot get along. Mr. Warren thought that he would take his time giving them Ruthie's address. He did not want to contaminate her because she worked at a doctor's office, they may try to coerce her into providing them with drugs.

Mr. Warren did follow Ruthie's life in a general sense, because he reached a point in his life when he regretted what he had done, but he could not undo any of it without incriminating himself. He was on the verge of having her return home after that incident with the Brenes, but then he started having problems with the other children. He just let that thought pass. Mr. Warren realized Ruthie's strength in dealing with issues and how capable she was in handling various situations. He never got any negative reports about her. There was always that group of people who had more positive things to say about her. Her attitude was good, school work was excellent, behavior good and so on............

After Ruthie got settled in her apartment she took a bus out to see Mrs. Carter's sister and niece. Greta was very happy to see her. They sat andchat for a while. Greta told Ruthie that the house was hers and she would gather her things and move out as soon as she can find a place. She said her mother (Mrs. Carter sister) told her and her family were only allowed to stay there and maintain the upkeep of the house until you are able to take over. She wanted her to know that her sister and husband wanted her to have the house but had not had the time to make it official. Greta's kids came in and was introduced to Ruthie. They hung around for a few minutes. They show their mother and Ruthie some things they made at camp and were going to hang them in their rooms. When they said their rooms, that triggered something in Ruthie's mind. (Their rooms) She thought for a moment and realized, it was no way she could ask them to give up their home. What does she know about taking care of such a large home? Her plans are to go to college and find her place in life when she complete college. A house this size is already taken and she is not sure what directions she will take in life. She just blurted out. "Look Greta, I want you and your family to keep this house, this house belongs to you and your family. This is the only home your children ever knew, am I right?"

"Yes, in a way, but we just moved in to maintain it until you were able to take over."

"Well, I am still not able to maintain it because I will be going to college for a number of years and will not be able to give it the love and care you and your family can."

"Look Ruthie, we will pay you so much each month. In fact, we can give you a few thousand dollar right now."

"No, the house is yours and your family. Please I don't want one penny from you. It's a gift from your Aunt, from me because they were my real parents for three years. When they died, I felt like dying. They taught me so much. I believe they are the reason I am here today."

"Ruthie, do you know the value of this home in this area" ?

"Yes, I can surmise, but I will not give it a second thought and that's that. The house is your"

"Ruthie, I now know why my Aunt loved you so much. Thank you. My husband is going to go berserk when I tell him what you did."

"Just tell him I love all of you very much for the time I was apart of your family."

Ruthie left and went back to her apartment. She pull out some brochures trying to determine what college she want to go too. Mrs. Connors had recommended the one she went too and that would mean she had to find another apartment closer. The next day she got on the telephone and made an appointment and if she liked it she would put out some feeler to search for and apartment close be it.

CHAPTER 5

Ruthie's thoughts were interrupted by two of her children who came home to see if she needed any more help in preparing for her wedding the next day.

"Hi, Mother."

"Hi, sweethearts."

"Okay, what else can I do to help? Did the dress fit alright? Come on, try it on so I can see you in it."

"It is fine Lois, I tried it on when Amber came in before. Tell her Amber, how it looked."

"Oh no, I don't trust anyone's judgement, but my own, especially where my beautiful mother is concerned. Come on lady, put it on."

"Oh for Pete sake, I don't know what to do with you."

"Mommy, just try the dress on so I can see how you are going to look tomorrow for Doctor. Todd Raine. Mother, that man is nuts about you. Amber isn't Mother beautiful. I bet if Daddy could see her now he would wish he never let her go. Now tell me Amber, can your sister sew?"

"Mother, isn't she facetious?"

"Quite."

"Mo------ther"

"Honey, I meant no disrespect. It is a compliment and it will be just between the three of us. Now sweetheart help me, I don't want to get it dirty or you will be all night making me another one exactly like this."

"Mother, do you know where we just came from?"

"No, where?"

"We were over at Todd's house. Mother, it is beautiful. He is making so many changes. It is not quite ready yet, but it will be when you two return from your honeymoon."

"How come he let you girls see it? He will not let me pass the front door."

"He wants it to be a surprise."

"Maybe I won't like it."

"Mom, even if you don't like the house, which I know you will, when Todd wraps those arms around you, you won't be able to notice the house anyway."

"Amber, take your conceited, fresh, little sister out of here before I put her across my knees and spank her." Amber and Lois got up and stood before their mother.

"Mommy, we love you."

"Don't try to get out of it." Ruthie put her arms around her two daughters.

"Boy do I love you gals. I am going to miss you. You know I have never been away from home a whole month. What am I going to do?"

"Mother, just enjoy your new life, as far back as I can recall, you earned it. You and dad raised all of us and made sure we kept our heads on straight. We love you very much and we want the best for you."

"Mom, did you talk to dad? What does he think about you marrying Todd?"

"No, Amber, I haven't heard anything from him. Weren't you and Troy Jr. over to see him a few times lately?"

"Yes, he just asks a lot of questions. When was the wedding, the time and place, etc, etc."

"Mom, do you think Dad is going to let you marry someone else? I know he still loves you."

"And how do you know that? Honey, he was the one who wanted a divorce. I was hoping we would get back together. But he said, "We might as well get a divorce. I thought that was what he wanted. You see I love Daddy very much and I thought it was my fault he started drinking so much. I don't know what I did nor why he drank so heavily. He left and went to stay with your grandma and he asked for a divorce. What was I to do? If a person stops loving you. Why try to hold onto them. If they are happy with someone else, I will not try to force them to love me. We all deserve to do what will make us happy. As much as I love someone I will let them go, without a fight. One thing you must alway remember to never fight over a man because if they want you, they would not be out there trying to talk and encourage a relationship with another woman." Lois was a bit frustrated about the conversation, so she spoke up.

"Look Amber, stop questioning mom about Dad because that is beside the point, she will be marrying Todd tomorrow."

"Lois stop yapping and let's help Mom get this place in order. We have to pick up the others."

"Okay Amber, Okay." It only took about fifteen minutes to put everything in place because Ruthie never allowed her house to remain untidy for long. The children were taught at an early age to help one another and always replace things.

After they finished straightening up, Lois went to pick up their two brothers from the airport and Amber went to the train station to get the other two children who had been visiting friends about a hundred miles away. Ruthie was alone again for a little while.

CHAPTER 6

Ruthie thought about the hundred thousand dollars from the Carters and the thirty thousand she had saved over the years in order to start her college career. She stayed in the apartment until she finalized her plans for college. She found an apartment close to the college. This time it was a little larger. Two bedrooms, a full bath, kitchen, sitting room, plenty of closet space and a small room on the side with a washer and dryer. It was located over the garage of a private home, owned by a couple with three children. The oldest boy attending the same college Ruthie would be attending, a fourteen year old girl and a eleven year old who suffer from a rare form of leukemia. Her name was Carrie, Susan and Troy the son. Carrie's condition was stable most of the time if she stayed with her diet and activities. She tends to be out of school more than she was in. Carrie was never allowed to be left alone and Troy was her main sitter.

The Thompsons wanted someone with Carrie, at all times. Susan was in high school and Troy a senior in college.

The Thompsons kept the apartment especially, to rent out to college students each year. The rent helped a great deal with the medical expenses for Carrie. They never knew when another bill would come.

Doctor Connor knew the Thompsons indirectly when he did his internship at the hospital when they first brought her in. Carrie was not his patient, but his co-workers. They were discussing her case when he asked to review her records. Based on Carrie's symptoms and test results, Dr. Connors had diagnosed her as having leukemia, however, they did not pick up on it until about a year later. One of his co-workers called to tell him when they finally made the diagnosis. Doctor Connors was black and an intern, plus, Carrie was not his patient. So, no one took his diagnosis seriously.

The Thompsons had fairly good insurance however, there was only so much the insurance would cover. By renting the apartment out, the added income was there for whatever came up.

Troy was devoted to his family and quite spoiled in many ways. He was the oldest and the only boy and the age difference between him and Susan was so that he was the only child for quite a while. Although, a lot was expected of Troy. His parents expected him to be around to help out with his sisters when they weren't there. Troy was expected to babysit Carrie because of her illness when his parents went out for the evening. He never complained to his parents about it, but he didn't like the idea. He would not argue with them...... He just did what he thought he should do regardless of what they told him.

Ruthie met Troy when she went down to find out about putting a small air condition in the apartment. Troy had brought his girlfriend by, after registering for class. They were going away for the weekend.

"Mother, I would like you to meet Lisa Graham, we are going out for a while and I may not be back until tomorrow."

"I am sorry Troy, but I need you to be here with Carrie because your Dad and I have to attend a banquet tonight."

"But, Mother, you know I was planning on going away for the weekend. My plans are all set."

"Troy, you know I don't want to leave Susan here alone."

"Mother, you will only be gone for a few hours and Susan will know where to reach you. She can do the same thing I would do, if I were here."

"Honey, but I would feel more comfortable if you were here. Now don't give me a hard time. You and Lisa can leave when we return." Mrs. Thompson turned to Ruthie.

"Oh Troy, I would like you to meet Ruthie K. Warren. she will be renting the apartment for..." Ruthie cut in. "For as long as you will let me."

Troy was a little too upset to notice Ruthie at that moment. Ruthie saw the hurt on Troy's face as well as the embarrassment. She decided to go to his rescue.

"Mrs. Thompson, may I talk to you privately, for a moment?"

"Sure, we can talk in the kitchen, if you don't mind."

"Mrs. Thompson, as you know, I will be studying nursing and I have worked in a Doctor's office for almost two years. I had various training in first aid and other general skill training in the care of patients. I would be more than happy to sit with the girls when I am not at work or in class, if you like. I don't know anyone here, so I have nothing to do. I plan to look for another job in a doctor's office as soon as I get settled. I am free tonight."

"Well, maybe you would be more qualified. You sure you would not mind? I will pay you."

"No, no, no, no pay. I would be more than happy to do it. It would be better than sitting upstairs twiddling my thumbs." Mrs. Thompson, followed by Ruthie, returned to where the others were.

"Carrie, this young lady volunteered to sit with you tonight. How does that sound?"

"Great Mom. I think she is nice. Mom, she is smart, she helped me this morning with my math." Carrie directed her attention to Ruthie said

"Ruthie, can we finish those other problems?"

"Sure, if you don't get too tired. I am going to do a little shopping now, if someone will point me in the direction of a good supermarket." Troy spoke up to show his appreciation.

"Hey, thanks, you saved the day. I want you to meet my friend, Lisa. I will drop you off at the market, if you are ready."

"I'll run up and get my purse." Troy took a good look at Ruthie and thought, "Man she is gorgeous."

Ruthie purchased a good supply of food and some other necessary things she felt she would need and took a taxi back to the apartment and by the time she cooked, ate and organized her food stuff, it was time to sit with Carrie and Susan. Although, Susan did not need a sitter.

Ruthie helped both girls with school work, they played games and she played the piano while they sang. The Thompsons came home at about eleven. They did not hear them come in because Ruthie was teaching Carrie to play a few notes on the piano. Carrie was so overjoyed with her ability to catch on so fast.

"Okay young ladies, it is past your bedtime."

"Sorry we lost track of time, Mrs. Thompson. Did you have a good time?"

"'Yes Ruthie and thank you."

"And you are more than welcome. Mrs. Thompson I have another question I would like to ask you."

"Sure, what is it?"

"I want to know if I can keep the apartment until I finish college, because I have no other place to go?"

"Where are your parents?"

"My mother passed away and my father remarried. I have not been living with them since I was a young child. Just recently I had my own apartment."

"I know, Doctor Connors before you moved in. I also spoke to him right before I left. I was hoping you would stay. You know they are very fond of you."

CHAPTER 7

●••••••••••••••••••••••••••••••●

Nobody had to tell Ruthie about having people in and out of the apartment. She took it for granted that it was not the right thing to do by bringing strangers around the Thompson's home, especially when the two young girls were usually around.

Ruthie found a part- time job in a local Doctor's office, not too far from where she lived. She worked only twenty hours weekly and on rare occasions twenty- five when they asked her. It was enough hours for her because of the number of credits she was taking at the college. She rarely went out because of her studies. She earned enough to cover the cost of her living expenses and did not have to touch her savings.

Troy had started to stay home a lot more as well as wait around to take Ruthie to her first class. Normally, he would leave as soon as he ate breakfast, even if his class started at one o'clock. Most times Ruthie would walk to the college it was only three blocks away.

Ruthie became the official sitter for Carrie and if she wasn't available, Carrie would pout and give Troy a hard time.

One night when Troy had to stay home with Carrie, she gave him such a hard time. When Troy saw Ruthie's light go on, he went up and asked her to give him a hand. Ruthie had a good habit of locking her door,

Even though she never had a problem at the Thompson's, she still locked it after going in and out.

Troy knocks on the door.

"Yes, who is it?"

"Ruthie, it's Troy." She opened the door to see what he wanted, not inviting him in.

"I came to ask a favor."

"Is something wrong?"

"Yes, will you come and talk to Carrie for me? She has been beside herself and I am climbing the walls."

"Sure, Tell her I will be right down, but first I must shower and change because the Doctor's office was full of sick people. There is some sort of virus going around."

"Okay, and thanks." Troy watched Ruthie when she spoke, he could see she appeared to be a little tired. However she still looked good to him.

Ruthie came down after she finished.

"What's wrong with my girl? Are you giving your brother a hard time?

"I miss you Ruthie. I haven seen you for five days."

"I am sorry. I have been working extra hours because a lot of people were out sick and I had my classes to attend. Hereafter, I will make sure I come in and give you a big hug at least every other day and on weekends and sometimes, maybe we can get to play a game or two. Okay?"

"Okay, Ruthie. Ruthie, will you show me how to play that song on the piano again?"

"Sure, come on, sit right here. Now put your fingers there and....."

Troy sat back and watched Ruthie. He was becoming more attracted to her. Mr. and Mrs. Thompson had taken Susan to a school program out of town and were not expected to return until late. Troy was quite appreciative for Ruthie's company because he had not been dating anyone lately, nor did he wanted to. He had his eyes on Ruthie. He was unsure of how to approach her. He certainly did not want to appear overly anxious or fresh. She was kind of special to him and was so different from the other girls he knew. He was good looking and he knew it, yet Ruthie never appeared to be interested in him. Ruthie was beautiful and all her curves were in the right places. Troy had wanted to ask her out for quite a while, but did not know how. Now that she was doing him a favor, by helping him with Carrie, he knew this was the opening he needed.

"Ruthie, how about a movie tomorrow night?"

"I have to work a little late."

"Well, what about the first night you are free?"

"Okay."

"I hope your boyfriend won't mind." Ruthie looked over at Troy and smiled.

"If your girlfriend won't mind, neither will my boyfriend."

"By the way, who is he?"

"I don't know. Between my classes and my job, I don't take time to socialize. I use my breaks on campus to study. I am trying to complete four years in three."

"What's the rush?"

"I was thinking about becoming a doctor. I am not sure yet. I am anxious to complete my education, wherever it ends and go on to the next phase of my life."

"You seem to be doing alright for yourself, why rush? You are also a very attractive person. Some of the guys are going whacked over you and they are very interested in meeting. I told them you are well cared for."

"Ha-ha-ha, why did you say that?"

"Do you want to meet them?"

"No, not really, just leave it the way it is."

Carrie had picked up on the notes quite well and was playing them over and over. The more she played the better she got.

"Carrie, that is great. If I am not too late tomorrow I'll teach you some more. I think it is time for you to go to bed."

"Okay, Ruthie. Good night."

"Night, sweetheart."

"Goodnight Troy, I am sorry about the way I acted."

"Okay, honey, good night." Ruthie picked up her things and headed for the door.

"I will be leaving now. Good night Troy." Troy stood up.

"Do you have to leave right away? I thought maybe we could talk."

"Maybe another time. Good night."

Ruthie had been living there for almost a year. Troy had tried to approach Ruthie and asked her out but she alway evaded him. It seem as if she knew he wanted to ask her out and she didn't want to be asked out. She kind of felt drawn to him. She felt like his eyes seem to follow her around. She had stop going into the house when he was around. She could never forget Bob Brene she kept her distance when she could, or seem to believe someone was staring at her, the way Bob Brene did. When she start living their Troy seemed like a big brother to her but that has changed. She liked Troy but only as a big-brother-friendly -person. She had no desires for a close relationship with him or anyone else, she had her studies to think about. She did not want a "Boy friend, or husband until she finish college. Her plans were in place and she did not want them interrupted.

CHAPTER 8

"Hi Mom." Ruthie was happy to see her boys.

"Hi, Troy, Larry. How is school?"

"Fine, is everything all set for the big day?"

"As soon as my other loves get here, I will be able to answer that question. Amber went to pick them up."

Ruthie watches the boys as they flop down on the couch. Troy Jr was the splitting image of his father. Just as tall and handsome. Just watching him, took her back to when Troy Senior began to really notice her and they started dating.

Ruthie remembered how she was taught by the foster care parents she loved so much, to be honest. She knew she did and could not give Todd the love and respect he deserved. She knew she could not go through this marriage. Her love for Troy still existed, even through they were not together. She believed he still loved her, but somewhere in the process, his parents were the reason they are not together. According to her children, Troy never went out with any other women, he merely drank alcohol, went to work, and stayed in his room at his parents' home. Their children accepted Todd and respected him because they were angry with their father and grandmother for allowing him to stay there. They knew their mother was hurting and missed their dad. They knew she never did anything wrong. Ruthie believe that her children encouraged marriage to Todd and if their father knew about it, he would 'wake up' and come home. Ruthie knew her children loved their father very much. He was always there for them. Ruthie decided to call Todd and call off the marriage. Because of the love he had for her, she believed it was real, but she could not return it and that was unfair to him. What man would prepare a place for a woman and six children, if he did not truly love her?

Todd was a handsome, successful doctor who could have his pick from many other unattached women, without children, but he chose her. Ruthie knew she liked him but was not in love with him. She could never bring herself to allow him to kiss her. A kiss from him was always on her forehead or cheeks. I guess he felt that once they were married, everything else would follow.

Ruthie picked up the telephone and dialed Todd's number. This kind voice answered. "Hello"

"Todd, it's Ruthie."

"I know Honey."

"Todd."

"Yes?"

"I want to apologize. You know I have a lot of respect for you and my intentions were never to hurt you, but I do not feel it would be fair to you for us to get married."

"Why? I love you very much."

"That I believe, but I may not be able to return the same love. Please don't be angry with me. However, if you do I will understand. I feel that there are so many women out there, without children or have fewer children than I have would make your life a lot easier and you would have more time to spend with her. I cannot envision what life would hold for us. I have so much to contend with and I don't think it is fair to you to bring all of my responsibilities to you and have their father in and about from time to time. I am sorry it took so long for me to make these decisions, but, and please understand. I also want you to know that my children love and respect you very much and they love their father very much and are in constant contact with him as well as wanting him to come home."

Ruthie was being Ruthie and she could never told Todd, 'I love you'. She respects him, but she loves Troy.

Ruthie was glad she got that off her mind. She hoped that Todd understood. She could deal with the loneliness, she had for the past nine months. The divorce from Troy came as a shock but she dealt with that. Yet she felt much about life is wonderful. Looking at where she is today, six wonderful loving children who she loved very much and they love her. She knew she had to have done something right. She just felt that Troy was at his weakest moment, feeling sorry for his parents and relieving his sister Carrie of some of the responsibilities of caring for his parents.

He might be feeling because he is the oldest, he should be the person who is taking care of them. Ruthie knew Troy's mother did not like her. Her reasoning, she did not truly know. 'Because she was not brought up in a stable home?' Those were some comments she made a couple times. Well, you wonder, what's a stable home has to do with 'against all odds' your life is successful".

CHAPTER 9

L ater that week when the office closed for the day, Ruthie came home right after class. She had not taken Troy seriously when he suggested going out to a movie.

She liked Troy, more like a brother than a boy friend. Which was why she was shocked when he called to tell her to be ready at seven. Ruthie had fixed dinner, ate, cleaned up and was ready to sit down and study when the telephone ranged.

"Hello."

"Hi, all set, the movie starts at seven thirty, we can leave at seven, okay, bye now." Ruthie hung up the telephone and reluctantly got dressed.

She went down a few minutes early so she could spend a few minutes with Carrie.

Mrs. Thompson liked Ruthie because she was so quiet and respectful and also because Carrie and Susan were so fond of her. Ruthie had really helped both of her daughters bring up their grades in school and she encouraged Carrie a lot to lessen her self pity tremendously as a result of her illness.

Mrs. Thompson had hoped Troy would pay more attention to Ruthie because she was a hard worker and smart. She never stayed out late at night. She kept her apartment neat and cleaned. Yet she did not want him to get too serious about her, such as marrying her. She felt she would be a good person to have some fun with until he find the girl he wanted to marry. Ruthie was very much different than the others who rented from them in the past years. The year Ruthie lived there she kept them abreast and up-to-date on any new development on treatments and cures which might benefit Carrie. Mrs. Thompson would always discuss those finds with Carrie's doctors.

Ruthie rang the doorbell, as she always did. Mrs. Thompson blurted out. "Come on in, how many times have I told you it was not necessary to ring the doorbell?"

"Oh, Mrs. Thompson, I suppose it is just a habit. Where is my little girlfriend?"

"She is somewhere around here." Ruthie went in to look for Carrie and found her passed out on the floor. She called out to Mrs. Thompson. "Mrs Thompson, come quickly, we must get her to the hospital.. fast. I will hold her, you call the hospital and let them know we are on our way."

Troy, hearing all the commotion came out to assist after finding out the reason for it.

Ruthie felt that the time they waited for the ambulance, they could take her to the hospital.

She could see the tears in Mrs. Thompson's eyes.

Ruthie had made a point in learning a lot about the various types of leukemia since being around Carrie for such a long period of time.

"She will be alright, don't worry." After they reached the hospital, Ruthie stayed right with Carrie the whole time comforting her and helping the doctors. A lot of the doctors knew her from the college where they lectured and the Doctor where she worked. Ruthie felt sad for Carrie, it was the first time she had a relapse since she moved there. When she came out of the room, after getting Carrie settled she could no longer hold back the tears. She leaned her head against Troy's chest and cried. He put his arms around her. When she got a hold on herself she apologized.

"I am sorry Troy, I just could not hold back the tears, they just came."

"That's okay, I understand." Still holding her, Ruthie stepped back. Troy let his hand slide down touching her hand and held onto it.

"Want to catch the late show, we still have time?"

"No, I'll rather stay here a little longer."

"Okay, me too." When Mr. and Mrs. Thompson came out, Troy, still holding Ruthie's hand, went in because Carrie was asking for them.

"Hi, Baby, how do you feel?"

"Okay now, can I go home?"

"No, I think the doctors will want to keep you here for a few days for observation. By the way

Young lady, I believe you did something I told you never to do and that could be why you are here, right?"

"Yes, and please don't tell Mommy. You won't, will you?"

"But, you must tell the doctor, okay?"

Carrie was kept in the hospital for five days. Ruthie visited her everyday at different times. Carrie was always watching for her because she told her about what time she would be there the following day. After Carrie came home and the household was back to normal, Troy saw a chance to try for another date, the day she came in to say hello to Carrie.

"Hi Mrs. thompson, I hear Carrie getting down with that piano. You know she is really smart and catches on fast."

"That is not what the teachers used to say." Ruthie smiling said. "Well, what do they know? Some people don't take time to see some people as people."

When Troy heard Ruthie talking to his mother he came out of his room. "Hi, Ruthie, how about a movie tonight?"

"That sounds great. Let's take Carrie, if it's alright with your mom." Very reluctantly, Troy responded, "Sure, if that's what you want." Gaining a bit of confidence. "Also on one condition, if you take a ride with me after we bring Carrie home."

Ruthie was beginning to feel more comfortable around Troy and had some feelings for him, much more than brotherly but did not want to admit. She was aware how he watched her and was sure it wasn't in a sisterly way. She did not feel she was ready for love and marriage

And anyway what would a guy like Troy want to spend the rest of their life with her. He came from a good upstanding family, had a very good education and a meaningful job. To be as young as he was, he was earning a very good salary. Ruthie felt she was comfortable with who she was but has not established herself yet. She had goals to reach, she did not want to be tied down to anyone, right now. She did not want to appear to be overly anxious to go out with him. She had a feeling that Mrs. Thompson was trying to get them together. She was always saying "Troy, why don't you take Ruthie with you to the game, club, or over your friends, etc, etc."

When he asked, Ruthie would always have something else to do. There were times he would invite her to go and she would always have something else to do and many times she would take in a movie alone.

She was aware of how Troy watched her, which was why when she visited Carrie she tried to make sure his parents were there or Troy was not there. She liked him but she did not want to like him enough to have an involved relationship with him.

Carrie enjoyed the movies very much, but not so much the movie, but that someone thought so much of her to suggest taking her out. Her respect for Ruthie grew immensely.

Most times her parents would say "Oh, no, that might upset her" or," I don't want to expose her that".

" Always some excuse not to take her places. It seemed like everything was "she can't do this or that because.."

After they brought Carrie home and said their goodnights, Troy took Ruthie to a Club where many college professors and graduate students hangout. On their way he told Ruthie how much he appreciated what she had done.

"Ruthie, you made my sister very happy tonight by suggesting the movie for her."

"Oh no, she must thank you and your mother for allowing her to go."

"I will argue with you on that because my first thought was, no, I wanted to take you out, alone."

Ruthie had anticipated that one day she probably would go out on a date with someone, so she had called Mrs. Leys to get a few answers to some questions on dating. She didn't know when but she felt 'one day'. She just wanted to be prepared.

"Hello, Mrs. Leys, this is Ruthie, I want to ask you a few questions, if you don't mind?"

"Ruthie? Could this be K. Warren?"

"Yes, this is she."

"I am so glad to hear from you." Ruthie went on giving her an update on what she was doing. They discussed the Brenes, Crossleys, and the Carters. Ruthie asked about Marlo. Marlo had run away from where she was placed back to the Brenes. She was there long enough to get pregnant. Tom beat her up so bad, she almost lost the baby. She was now living on her own, working and attending a trade school with the help of welfare.

"It's so funny Ruthie, she asked about you last week."

"When you see her, tell her I am still a virgin." If I had her address, I would like to visit her or call her sometime. Why don't you give her my address and phone number, even though she may still be angry with me."

"I don't think she is angry with you, she has a lot of respect for you. When are you coming to visit us?"

"I will try when I get on Spring Break and can get a day off from my work." Ruthie had always had a lot of respect for Mrs. Leys because she was always fair in her dealings with the issues affecting her. They discussed dating and things to avoid, such as alone in dark places, bedrooms, backseats in cars, prolonged necking and hugging, rooms with couches and alone in isolated places.

CHAPTER 10

··

When Ruthie and Troy walked into the Club, right away a couple of the guys approached them and invited them to join them. Troy introduced Ruthie. She had seen most of them on campus and they her. She had class with a couple of them, but never had a conversation with any one of them. She was always in and out of class having no time to hang around and talk. If she was involved in activities on campus she would fulfill her assignment and leave. Many times she would take parts in shows put on by the drama club, sing, play the piano or whatever they needed her for.

The Guys were in the process of ordering drinks. "You two are just in time to order a drink. This place is so busy it takes a while to place and order. What will you have, Ruthie?"

"Seven-up on the rocks." Ruthie gave them a broad smile and expected a reaction.

"Ah, come on, you can do better than that."

"Troy, how about you order for the lady?"

"Man if she said seven-up, then it's seven-up."

"Okay.. Seven-up coming up."

Troy had one drink while the other guys had at least two or three while they were there.

The Club had a live band and the floor was crowded with couples dancing to the fast music. When the music mellowed, Troy asked Ruthie to dance. He held her so tight, she could barely move. Ruthie looked up at Troy with a troubled smile, as she spoke.

"Troy, I thought you asked me to dance?"

"Yes, I did."

"How can I when you are holding me so tight?"

"I can't help myself, I am very much in love with you."

"Troy, please don't say that."

"I must, I cannot hold it in forever." He released his hold on her, took her hand and led her outside. They walked over to the picnic area where many others were sitting, standing around talking, drinking, caressing and strolling around. Troy found a place where they would not be noticed and took Ruthie in his arms. Ruthie was so unsure of how to respond, because this was not what she wanted. She was afraid she could fall in love with Troy or have.

"No Troy, please take me home now."

"Okay, I will give you time to think about 'us'. Just remember, I love you very much and there is nothing you can say, or do, to change the way I feel about you." Ruthie said nothing. When she got in the car, she sat as far away from him as she could. Troy put the key in the initial and just sat there, not saying a word. After a few minutes Ruthie questioned him. "Is something wrong?"

"Yes, I am waiting for you to get in the car." He patted on the seat closest to him. Ruthie looked over at him, barely speaking his name. "Troy?" He responded. "I said, in the car." Ruthie moved over closer to him. He put his arms around her and drove off. When they got home he walked her to her door. "May I come in?" She felt that she just had the shock of her life and was not ready for anything else. No, I rather you didn't. She turned to put the key in the door. Troy gently turned her around and spoke softly. "Then I'll kiss you goodnight right here. Ruthie turned her face, expecting him to give her a kiss on her cheek. Troy took one hand and turned her face enough to reach her lips. "Baby, I kiss my sisters and my mother on their cheeks, as for you, I want your lips." He kissed her gently and left.

For the next few days Ruthie did everything she could to avoid him. If she did not have to work late, she would go to the library and study. Study anything so she did not have to face Troy. If she thought it was time for him to come home, she would close her blinds and turn out the lights, pretending she was not at home. If the phone rang, she would not answer it, if it was Troy. This lasted for a couple of days. Troy knew she was trying to avoid him, so he drove his car down the street, parked it and walked back. When Ruthie saw his car left, she decided to go down to say hello to Carrie and Susan. When she rang the bell, Troy opened the door with a smile. Ruthie was a bit stunned.

"Hi, I haven't seen you around for the last couple days. Where have you been? And don't tell me you have been working because I've been to your job looking for you. Are you trying to avoid me? I am telling you now, it's not going to work."

"Troy."

"Yes, can we go out to dinner and dance tonight, because I am going to bother you until you do and if you try going out with any other guy, I am going to tell them you are my wife."

"I am serious Ruthie, I mean every word I say and have said. Now if you are ready for class, I will drop you off. I am not in a hurry to get to work on time today. I will take the day off if you tell me to." Ruthie got her things and walked to the car with Troy. Once in the car Troy put his arms around Ruthie and gently kissed her. She knew she had to apologize for her behavior.

"I'm sorry Troy. I suppose I am confused. I was avoiding you. It's just that, when I fall in love, I want to be sure."

"So do I. Can we go out tonight? And we will not be taking Carrie this time, understand?"

"Yes, (looking over at Troy and smiling) but why not, that sounds like a good idea, I am sure she would like another night out." Troy pulled the car over and came to a complete stop, when he heard what Ruthie said. He took her in his arms. "Do you want to fight me now? Are later. I am not going to move this car until you prove to me that you are not serious." Ruthie burst out laughing. "I was only joking."

"Are you sure?"

"Quite." Troy started the car and proceeded to drop Ruthie off to the campus. He had made up his mind that before Ruthie got out of his car today she was going to show him some affection. She was going to return his kisses in a meaningful way. When he pulled up to the curb, immediately she reached for the door. Troy took her arm, "Aren't you forgetting something?"

"What?"

"My goodbye kiss."

"Oh Troy, please." She made another attempt to get out of the car.

"What did I say, Baby? I am serious." Ruthie gave him a quick peck on his cheek.

"Oh no, you will not get away that easily, I believe you have a short memory. He kissed her passionately. Ruthie could feel her feelings for Troy coming alive. She had never in her life experienced anything like that before. She was frightened. Her mind reverts back to her life plans and her childhood. She must not allow anything to change that. She had come too far to allow her feelings for someone to interrupt her years of planning for her education and her life. Sure she wanted a loving husband, children, and happiness, but will Troy love her enough? Will he place demands on her to put aside her plans? She had a lot of thinking to do before she made any real permanent commitments, regardless of her feelings for him.

After that kiss, Troy was sure she cared. What he felt for her, he knew she felt the same way about him. "We are going out tonight. Be ready at six. Will that be time enough for you? Love you.

CHAPTER 11

About a quarter to six, Troy was knocking on Ruthie's door. She was all dressed and ready to go. She made sure of that because she did not want Troy lingering in her apartment alone too long with her. Ruthie was unsure of where they were going for dinner and dancing so she decided to go all out and purchase a dynamite outfit for the occasion. Troy had never seen her really dressed up before, for an evening out because she never went out much, only for a movie or a Broadway show every now and then with the students at college. For that no one wore anything special.

Ruthie purchased a white chiffon dress with an oval shaped neckline. The dress was gathered slightly around the waist and the bottom of the hem lining causing it to puff, earring and bracelet to match with a touch of baby blue mixed. Ruthie was a very beautiful girl. If beauty, knowledge and talent was the only thing to become Miss America for any year, she would be the winner.

When Troy walked in, every part of him became excited by what he saw.

"Hel.. lo, Ba.. by, wow, uh, uh."

"Hi, Troy, I am ready, if you are?

"Can we stop by the Preacher and get married before we go to dinner and then can come back and start our honeymoon?"

"I truly believe you are sick, let me check your temperature." When she reached up to touch his forehead, Troy could not help but to take her in his arms, he gently kissed her and then just held her.

"Troy, please don't."

"Why?"

"Because I think it is time to go."

"Why?"

"Because I am hungry."

"I bet."

"Troy."

"Are you afraid to tell me you have fallen in love with me and we should get married right away?"

"Yes and no, in a way."

"What kind of answer is that?"

"It's the only one I can think of, at this moment."

"One thing I must say is that you are honest and another thing, if you don't marry me soon, I don't know if I can survive this boyfriend, girlfriend relationship."

"Troy we must have patience and not rush into anything, please? I have a lot of things I must consider and think through before marriage. Please understand?"

"What more to think and consider, I love you and want you to be my wife, now, and that's all that matters."

Ruthie knew that, that was not all that mattered to her, she had a lot to overcome and she had to find out how. She just could not allow herself to be absorbed in Troy's way of thinking and doings, she had to consider her ways in the pursuit of life. His upbringing was so much different than hers. Troy must understand those things. When you commit yourself to a lifestyle you must be aware of all the possible outcomes. Troy has a family and his parents are very protective of him and to a great degree, controlling. They expect him to 'jump' when they tell him. Ruthie noticed a change in them when he began paying a lot of attention to her.

She got along well with them as long as she was doing things which pleased their needs. They wanted him to become a little serious about her, but only if they could control what was going on. Ruthie felt that she could almost read a person's actions and means at times.

Ruthie had always liked Troy, but she had no intentions of falling in love with him, but she did. Mr. and Mrs. Thompson alway appeared to like Ruthie very much and they were always trying to find ways to get her and Troy together their way

Troy took Ruthie to a nice Club where they had dinner and the entertainment was wonderful.

There was a floor show and after the floor show then the floor was cleared for dancing. Troy tried to get Ruthie to drink a small glass of champagne, but she refused. He had whiskey and soda. "Do you want something stronger" ? She said "No, a glass of ginger ale will be fine."

"What is it about alcohol you do not like?"

"Well, if it is not kept under control, it can ruin a family and the person itself."

"Look, I have taken a drink from time to time for years and it has not ruined my life."

"Why do you drink? How does it make you feel? Have you ever drank more than you knew you shouldn't have? A friend of mine said it made her feel offer, after a night of drinking. Also I knew of a family where too much alcohol caused them to lose their children, their home, their job and I often wonder to this day what happened to their children and them".

"I will tell you one thing, that will never happen to me, because I only drink socially and my system does not crave alcohol. My only craving right now is to wake up every morning and find you beside me in bed." Ruthie smiled. "I'll stick with my seven-up ginger ale or other kinds of soda and leave it to others who enjoy the taste of alcohol, because that's not for me. Some people said alcohol gives you a different outlook on things and it makes you feel kind of funny. I don't need anything to make me feel funny, I want to be funny on my own".

"Have you ever tasted alcohol?"

"Yes, I stuck my tongue in it one time and it tasted horrible."

Troy summoned the waiter and ordered a seven-up. The Waiter smiled, as if to say 'you got to be kidding'. They sat with a friend of Troy's from his job. Ruthie enjoyed the evening with them, the lady was pursuing a degree in law and expecting to finish within the next two years.

After dinner they went into the lounge where there was dancing. Ruthie stuck with her kind of drink and Troy merely sipped on the one he had, not ordering any other.

Troy led Ruthie to the dance floor. Once in his arms, Ruthie allowed him to hold her as close as he wanted without pushing him away. The music changed from slow to fast without them noticing. Troy whispered, "Will you marry me? And I will not accept anything but yes?"

Ruthie dropped her hands to her side and started to back to their table. He took her hand, and stood in front of her.

"Am I getting a brush off?"

"No Troy,..... I"

"I what?"

"I want to think about it."

"We had this conversation before, what's there to think about?"

"I must, please?"

They sat quietly through another part of a show and then left. Troy wanted to take her anywhere but home. He wanted to just hold her in his arms, but soon realized that he was quite limited to how far he could go with his new found love Ruthie Katrina Warren.

"Honey let's go someplace where we can be alone, I just want to get close to you?"

"Troy, I think we are close enough, right now, because I don't want you to get any ideas that you will get any closer, understand?" I love you too but no."

"Why?"

"Because I said so."

"That is not a good enough reason?"

"You mean to tell me that you do not respect my opinions about our relationship?"

"I have a right to try to change your opinions, Don't I?"

Ruthie tried to push him away but it was hopeless, so she slid her arms around his neck. They stood caressing and kissing forever, so long. Finally Troy thought he had her where he wanted and she could not deny him anything.

"Baby, we are going where we can be alone for the rest of the night, okay?"

"No Troy, we are not going to sleep together, please take me home."

"Baby I can't." Tears begin to flow from Ruthie's eyes. Through her tears she tried to make him understand. "I love you Troy, but I don't want us to start out that way, please understand?"

Still holding her close. "Okay Baby, I don't want to try to understand, but because I love you, I will do as you asked. Please stop crying. I am going to kiss you until every tear disappears."

Troy wanted to get married right away and Ruthie wanted to finish college however that was almost two years and he did not want to wait that long.

"I have to do a lot of thinking about that. You are the woman I want and I am not going to wait two years. Now you think about that and come up with some solution. I love you Ruthie."

After Troy took Ruthie home that night, he lingered around at the door until she asked him in.

"Troy, would you like to come in for a glass of juice? it's senseless to just stand out there." Troy readily accepted. He still wanted to spend the night with her, by her asking him in, he thought maybe she changed her mind. Once inside he took her in his arms and kissed her. Ruthie knew he was getting a little carried away and she knew it was time for him to leave.

"Troy, please leave now."

Troy kissed her with all the passion he felt for her and left. When Troy got in the house he woke his parents up to tell them how much he was in love with Ruthie and wanted to marry her.

"Mom, Dad, she is in love with me, I knew it and she said so, but I can't understand why she doesn't want to marry me right now."

"What did she actually say? When you asked her to marry you?"

"She said she wanted to think and she wanted to finish college, but Mom, that is about another two or three years and I don't want to wait that long."

"Honey, maybe she wants to be sure she is making the right decision. Maybe she has been hurt before."

"Mom, I don't think so. You know she has never drunk anything alcoholic before and would not drink anything tonight? I have never been so much in love with one woman before as I am with Ruthie. I guess you know I have been liking her for a long time, but I also wanted to be sure and it is not just sexually because she will not let me get that close. She moves me in all kinds of directions. I used to get angry with girls when they would not do whatever I asked of them, but with Ruthie I find myself trying to understand when she says no and going along with her decisions. Dad, is this the way women treat men when they are so much in love with them?"

"Well, son, your Mom gave me the run around before she agreed to marry me."

"Then it is normal for women to respond that way?". They all laughed. Troy apologized for waking his parents and went off to bed, but very little sleep he got that night.

Troy got up after about an hour, put on his robe and went to Ruthie's apartment, started to knock on the door, but changed his mind and went back to bed. He did manage to get about two hours sleep that night, or I should say morning, just before it was time to get up and go to work.

That morning he waited for Ruthie to come down before he left. He knew she always came in to see Carrie before she went off to school herself.

Ruthie had a very restless night. She was disturbed about her feelings for Troy. She believed she was in love with him, but she didn't want to make any commitments before she learned a little more about life. She did not want to see Troy this morning, but she knew she could not keep running away, so she got dressed, had her breakfast and went down. Troy was sitting at the table, sipping coffee when she walked in.

"Good morning, Folks, where is my girlfriend? Troy looked up, wanting to hold her in his arms, even if it was for a few moments.

"Aren't you going to ask about how I am?"

"No, because I know you are alright."

"And how do you know that? '

"By just looking at you." Troy stood up. "I want you to check my forehead and make sure because I am not sure I feel so hot." Troy took Ruthie's arms and attempted to put them around his neck when Carrie walked in.

"Hi, Ruthie, I thought I heard you come in. Did you have a good time with my brother last night?"

"Yes, I had a very good time."

I wish you would marry my brother then you could sleep in his room. I always miss you when you say goodnight and go up to that apartment alone, but I am glad you were the person to rent it. Sometimes I wonder if you had not come here what would I have done for a friend? I have been going to school now for almost a whole term without any problems.

"I am sure you would have been fine, you know you are very bright and sooner or later you would have realized it. We must become somewhat independent before we catch on to "life".

Remember how fast you picked up on those notes when I was teaching you how to play the piano? It wasn't me playing it was you."

"You are saying that to make me feel good." Carrie throws her arms around Ruthie.

Troy came over to Ruthie and put his arms around her. He had to go out of town to a conference and wanted Ruthie to come with him.

"I have something to ask you."

"Okay, shoot."

"I will tell you later when you get home from work."

"I have a few minutes, you can tell me now"

"I said later."

"Okay, later. I am out of here and on my way to work."

"Wait, I will drop you off."

"Are you sure you have the time?"

"For you, yes.

When Troy came home he went up to Ruthie's place, for dinner,. After dinner they sat down and talked about marriage that Ruthie felt she was not ready for. Ruthie tried to change the conversation.

"You said you had something to talk to me about, and I did not think it was marriage."

Oh, yes, I have to go out of town next week to a conference and would like for you to come with me."

"Well, I don't know about that, I would think about it if I had my own room."

"That could be arranged, if that is all you are concerned about."

"What day will we leave and return? I will see about taking time off from work, if it is necessary."

Troy fills her in with all the details. The next day when Ruthie got to work she let her boss know the days she would be off.

The next day, Ruthie informed Troy that she will be able to go. Troy was pleased, he had plans for them to be together with hope that he could get her to set a wedding date. Troy was truly in love with Ruthie so much so that he had not look at another women since Ruthie moved in their apartment in the back of their house.

Ruthie was interested in the conference because she was always looking for something to write about for her college papers. She was hoping she could get Troy to get her into a few of their sections. She like to write about the pros and cons of detail information. Ruthie wasn't looking to have a "good time" at the conference, she was seeking information to help her to boost her grades at college.

Troy had other ideas for him and Ruthie. Ones that Ruthie was not aware off.

When the meetings were done for periods of times all of the group were entertained with shorts trips, shows, music for dancing, dinners and snacks all around the facilities. No one could have been bored. Even when it was just the guest, they were well entertained.

Troy was constantly trying to get into Ruthie's room or she in his so they could spend some time together, any information she wanted he got it for her. She also was able to sit in some of the sessions.

The conference was well planned. All the men brought wives or significant others who shared their room. It seems like Troy and Ruthie were the only ones with single rooms. Troy tried his best to be with Ruthie but she refused. The last night they were there, he was so angry, he went into her room and refused to leave. He got in the bed and Ruthie slept on the chair. That morning he got up, went to his room, packed his things, came back and gave Ruthie fifteen minutes to get ready to leave. Ruthie told him to leave and she will find her way home.

After Troy left Ruthie hurried and check out the room, thinking he might feel sorry and return and apologize for becoming angry. Before to long she saw him came back to the room. She hid over in a corner out of sight. He went to the desk clerk and ask her some questions and he looked around for her but she remained out of sight. When she was sure he was gone she went down to the Desk Clerk and she helped her find transportation home.

She got home a bit late that night and she had an urgent message on her phone from Marlo.

CHAPTER 12

R uthie called Marlo, and when she answered, she was in tears.
"Ruthie I am so glad you called, I need some advice. Tom
came over to see his son. While he was here I had my rent money
on the dresser by the door. He was the only one in my apartment and when
he left the money disappeared. I did not see him take it. It was all I had
and I knew where I always put it in the same place, so when they came to
collect it, I just handed it to them. I am on a month to month lease. If I
don't pay, I have to move out in three day. I lost my job because Timmy
was sick and had no one to care for him. When a kid has a fever, day care
will not allow them to come. I have tried everywhere to see if I can get
some help, nothing anyone can do. All they say is 'come in and fill out an
application'. I just want to know if you know of any place where I can get
help immediately. I don't want my child taken away from me and placed in
foster care. You know what you went through in these foster-care homes."

"Marlo, do not put foster care homes down because there are many
loving homes who love and care for children as if they were their own. I
know that for a fact."

"Ruthie, I am so sorry for what I did to you by not telling the truth
and backing up what you said. I thought about that a lot. It seems like all

76

the things you were telling me happened." Marlo started to cry. Ruthie tried to calm her.

"Look, that's in the past. When do you have to move?"

"By tomorrow, I have to be out of this apartment."

"Marlo, give me your address, and I will be there as early as I can tomorrow and do not go anywhere until I get there, okay."

"I want you to start packing your things and cleaning up, okay."

"Ruthie, I do not have any money and I do not want to take my child in a shelter.

"Look Marlo, we will face that problem when I get there, understand? Just get packed, okay. Do you have something to pack your things in?"

"Yes.

"Okay, I will see you as soon as I can."

Ruthie got up early the next morning, went to the bank and drew out $10. 000. She put $5. 000 in her checking account and kept the other $5. 000 in her purse. She arrived at Marlo's place before noon. It seemed like the moment she touched the doorbell the door flung open.

Marlo threw her arms around Ruthie apologizing over and over, tears streaming down her cheeks. Ruthie eased away as she spoke.

"Marlo, I never held anything against you because you did what was right for you at that time. I'm okay with that. Let's begin to think about today and tomorrow." She reached for little Timmy.

"Hi Timmy, can I have a hug?" Timmy walked over to her with a smile.

"Okay-----pausing-----Ruthie," Marlo had never accumulated a lot of stuff. She had two very large suitcases and a couple small one. Ruthie called around trying to find a hotel where they could stay for a couple days, while trying to find an apartment. They had to get two taxis, one to carry her stuff and the other to carry them.

Marlo turned in her keys before she left and had someone to check everything out. When they got settled in the hotel Ruthie started calling around. Everybody wanted them to put in an application so they could run a check on the person. Then Ruthie thought about the Vargas's, where she got her first apartment. When she called Mrs. Vargas remembered her right away.

They never had any problem with Ruthie when she lived there, she always paid her rent on time, never any complaint, and when she left she left a lot of nice things. They offer to pay her for it but she said maybe someone may come along and need something and you might share

Marlo had gotten laid off from her job because of being out so long. So she called Mrs Brene to see if she could lend a helping hand and that was when she sent Tom over. When she called her about the missing money, Mrs. Brene cursed her out. Prior to that Marlo had been working a full time job, Timmy was in daycare and she did not have to pay. The State Welfare was helping some, she was also taking some night classes.

Ruthie explained the situation concerning Marlo. So she would know that in time Marlo will find a job, until then she would help her. Ruthie offered to pay Marlo's rent for the first six month and if she ran into a problem she was to let her know. Mrs. Vargas readily accepted Marlo. Mrs. Vargas told her the place would be ready the next day. They all stayed in the hotel that night and early the next day gathered all their things and again two taxis, instead of trying to lug all that stuff on a bus. The hassle of going by bus outweighs the cost of the two taxis.

When Ruthie was talking to Mrs. Vargas, Marlo was not paying any attention, the only part caught her attention was "I'll bring her tomorrow"

"Ruthie, are we going to some place tomorrow?"

"Yes, I found you and Timmy and an apartment."

"You found us a place?"

"Yes.

"But Ruthie. I don't have any money nor do I have a job."

"I know and she knows. You will have six month to work things out."

"But Ruthie, the rent."

"I said, you will have six month to work things out, okay?"

"Ruthie, can I go to sleep now? I want to make sure I am not dreaming because if you are here when I wake up then I will know what I just heard is true?"

"Okay Marlo, let's get something to eat first, okay?"

Close to the hotel they found a nice restaurant. Ruthie and Marlo talked a lot about life in general. Marlo talked about how much she wanted her son to be close to his family, that was why she tried to keep in touch with the Brenes. Ruthie responded.

"Look Marlo, why try keeping in touch with anyone that disrespect you. You don't need that. If they love Timmy they will reach out to you. They know your situation. If they want him a part of their life they would hunt you down. Timmy doesn't need a father who stole from him, who took away his bed, his home, who put him out in the street, who disrespect the only person who provides for him. Stop expecting anything from them or him. If he doesn't willingly support him, don't ask. When you move do not let them know where. If they want to know they will find you. Stop inviting them to holidays, birthdays are whatever else you have for Timmy. Stop worrying about your problems, just do something about them. I understood a long time ago that everything I went through was a test of my faith. We are supposed to be here on this earth and when problems arise we are supposed to handle them not buckle under, crying and mourning. We are supposed to stand tall and say "I GOT THIS" and "I AM NOT GOING TO LET IT GET ME". Remember who your "CREATOR" is, we did not create ourselves. Just start living a righteous life and things will workout for you. Stop blaming others for the things that did not go right in your life. What it may be, you had a choice, no one made you do what you did. You allowed others to make choices for you. You must take control of yourself at all costs.

I met a guy who I am very much in love with and he tries to make choices for me. He is angry with me right now but I care less, he is not going to make me do anything, I don't feel it's not right. If he quits me, so what, I know what direction I want to go. It's my way or the highway, it's his choice. In life we wait for many things, if we are hungry, we must wait until the food is done, if we are sick, we wait for the doctor when we work, we wait for our paycheck, in traffic, we wait for the light to change, women carry a baby in their stomach for nine month and have to wait while carrying that heavy load. Life is wonderful if we establish our priorities and not merely take the easy way out. Our wants and needs are basically the same but there is a time for everything. It's always best to wait and see if it is time for that want or need to materialize.

I have a lot of sympathy for my parents as well as the Brenes. I also sympathized with you back in the day because I knew you were so hung up on Tom and I was hoping but understood that you would not back me up nor stand by me. Why? Because Tom was your life. Also I was not surprised when he turned on you because he always had another girlfriend and was using you.

"Why didn't you tell me?"

"If I told you, you would not have believed me. The girl was named Elaine Grossman."

"What, that was who he married."

"Tom got married?"

"Yes, he sure did. They are still together. They married right after the trial.".

"Marlo, stop allowing people to use you because you are a child of someone special and mightier than anyone here on earth. Someone that groomed you to withstand the temptations of life and to prepare for the next. Didn't you ever listen to the messages when we went to church? You see, I listen and I read the scriptures to make sure I was understanding the right things."

"A little bit, but I was not into that church thing. Remember what you told the Pastor when he would not vouch for you at the trial and all the things you did at the church."

"I was merely a little orphan child in foster care. The Brenes were starch members for many years. I didn't expect him to say anything that would have offended The Brenes. I was only hoping he would have talked about all the positive things I did at the church, that would not have offended them. At that hearing I felt like the world was against me and I had to defend myself. Then I realized the world was not against me, only a few people and I was going to defend myself because I knew the truth nor did I care what others thought about me. The 'GOD' in me dried all my tears and I stood my ground. No one could see my friend but "HE" was right by my side. The teachers supported me, my boss supported me as well as my caseworker. I found out a long time ago that you cannot worry about what people say about you, if you watch people when they point their finger at you, if you notice, there are three pointing back at them. You might think they are defaming you but they are only talking about themselves. We must love life and smile when you are criticized because people are only commenting on things they are going through and trying to make you believe it's you. Marlo you may feel a bit out of place now, but hold your head up high and don't wear your problems on your shoulders. If you cannot accomplish something you set out to do, don't worry about it, set your mind on something else or pick up a pen and write about it and develop a solution.

You must always look forward to tomorrow and prepare for the future. When one thing does not go your way, try something else. There are different ways to reach each destination. There are many 'roadblock' (or ways) to reach your goals, sometimes we have to try them all before we accomplish what we set out to do. Never give up on life and life will not give up on you. Life challenges may be small or they may be large but do not let them get you down, just smile and move forward. Marlo I say these things because I went through most of them and am still being challenged. Right now you are faced with many issues but I know you are prepared to deal with them and you are going to come out on top. I want you to know I am here for you and you must feel free to call me anytime. I am sure one day Mr. Right will come your way and do not forget to invite me to the wedding.

Ruthie introduced Marlo to the Vargas's and they explained their rules and welcomed little Timmy. Mrs Vargas had her grandson in the office and he and Timmy hit it off right away.

The Vargas's live about two blocks away from their hotel and Mrs. Vargas babysits her grandson. When Ruthie heard that she mentioned "Mrs. Vargas do you baby sit other children?"

"Yes, sometimes."

"Maybe, when Marlo gets a job you might consider caring for little Timmy because it seems like those two has join forces already."

"Yes, I see that and my grandson can use some company close to his age. He has a sister but she is five years older and they are forever fighting." Ruthie commented.

"Marlo we came to the right place at the right time. We found a place for you the stay and a possible sitter for Timmy. We accomplished a lot in two day." Marlo smiled.

"Ruthie you accomplished a lot for us in two days and I do not know how I can repay you."

"Look Marlo, you do not own me anything, what I am doing is my gift to you and Timmy. I believe you have learned a lot over the years and you are ready to pursue life in a positive way and things are going to workout for you and Timmy. Just never believe all you hear, base your life on what you know to be right not what you think, You are a good person and good people do make mistake but once they realize their mistake they can be a much better person. Just remember, mothers and fathers are important in ones life but if they are not there you have to deal with who and whats there. You fill that void with other thing when someone is missing. It can be done.

CHAPTER 13

It seemed like the Thompson were angry with Ruthie because she did not allow Troy to sleep with her. When they found out why he left her at the conference prior to that they had begun to act differently toward her. Ruthie wondered how they felt when Troy told them he was in love with her and he had asked her to marry him. Lately she had notice a change in both Mr. Thompson and Mrs. Thompson When she spoke to them, they mumbled. Soon after Mrs. Thompson told her that she thought she should find another place because they were going to raise the rent. She did not know, Ruthie was already looking for another place. In fact, she had already found one.

Ruthie was quite confused at this point, she felt that parents were supposed to keep their children away from that kind of relationship..... not encourage it. As time passed, Ruthie gave up on ever renewing her relationship with Troy. She called Carrie as little as possible, because she did not want the Thompsons to think she was trying to find out what Troy was doing. Carrie would call often and keep her informed on Troy's relationships. She tried to discourage any mention of Troy, she would block the rest of the conversation out of her mind which was related to Troy. Troy had called her several times and wanted to talk, but she had very little to say to him. He apologized for his behavior and wanted to take her out but she was always busy. He came by her job when he thought she was leaving for the day and offered to take her home but she told him she had a class and a ride.

During the Summer months, work at the Doctor's office was rather slow and he closed the office for two weeks. Ruthie had plenty of time on her hands. Some of the ladies at the office got her to help with summer programs for youth. Ruthie fit right in with the program. She started contacting the businesses in the area to help get jobs for youth, planning a youth convention which included workshops, social activities and other things she felt would benefit the youth. Even with her busy schedule, she kept in contact with the Thompsons, especially Carrie. Mrs. Thompson had snubbed her more than once, but she looked past that because she promised Carrie that she would be her friend. The group she was working with was planning a city-wide convention and she wanted Carrie and Susan to come. Ruthie was taking a summer class at the college. After class, one day, she called Mrs. Thompson to see if she could come over. She agreed.

Mrs. Thompson was glad to talk to Ruthie because she had developed a strong dislike for the girls Troy was going out with. She was rude, had a flip lip and Carrie and Susan could not stand her. Also Mr. Thompson's tolerance was at the lowest ebb. Before Ruthie could knock on the door, Mrs. Thompson opened it. it was as if she was watching for her to come.

"Hi, Mrs. Thompson, Is Carrie home yet?"

"No, She won't be for another hour. How have you been?"

"Busy with the youth program. That's one reason I came by. I would like Carrie and Susan to come to our Big Event. Here is a copy of the program outline." Mrs. Thompson took the program and glanced over it, but she could not keep her eyes off Ruthie. She for once in her life had a good look at what her son saw in her. She was beautiful, respectful, honest, kind and quite innocent. She thought about how she treated her and she did not even bother to hold a grudge. "My Ruthie, what do you do with yourself? You are more beautiful than the last time I saw you. How do you manage that?"

"I work hard at not worrying about things I cannot change."

"Are you going out with anyone steady?"

"No, I really haven't gone out with anyone since Troy. I don't want to get hurt again. I loved Troy very much, but that's all over. I am glad he is happy now." They sat and chatted for quite a while. Shortly before it was time to pick Carrie up, Mrs. Thompson left the room and called Troy and told him that Ruthie was there and wanted to see Carrie and would he pick her up.

Ruthie realizing it was time for Carrie to be home said. "Mrs. Thompson, do you have to pick Carrie up?"

"Oh no, I called someone, she will be here in a few minutes."

When Carrie walked in and saw Ruthie, she threw her arms around her, Troy came in a few seconds afterward. Ruthie did not notice him at first.

"Alright, Carrie, enough is enough, it is my turn now." Troy was still very much in love with Ruthie. He only latched onto these other girls to spite his parents in hope it would make them appreciate Ruthie more. He had a fit when Ruthie moved out of the apartment.

Ruthie looked over at Troy, still standing with her arms around Carrie's shoulders.

"How have you been, Troy?"

"Do you want me to tell you the truth or a lie? I feel rotten, especially, because of what I did to you. I was being selfish, disregarding everything you stood for. I wish I could make up for what I have done. Is that possible?"

"Troy, don't give it a second thought." Turning to Carrie, she said, Carrie do me a favor, just save me a small slice of the wedding cake, deal? Carrie frowned

"What wedding cake?"

"Troy's and Delia's I must be going now."

"Can I talk to you for a few minutes, Ruthie? Troy was standing in front of her, blocking the door. "Please? Let me drive you home?"

I left my car at the school, because it is so hard to get a parking place over here."

"I am running kind of late..... if you don't mind and if Delia doesn't mind, I would appreciate it if you could drop me off at the High School across town because I have practice with the kids."

Troy tried to looked astonished, "You have a car? I didn't know you could drive".

"Oh yes, here, there was no place to park a car, that's why I never bought one."

Yes, Troy knew she had a car because he spent most of his spear time watching if anyone went in or out her place.

"Mommy, can I go with Ruthie to practice?" Please Mommy, Troy can pick me up later, can you Troy?"

"Carrie, you haven't as much as asked Ruthie yet."

"Oh, Mrs. Thompson, I would love to have her. She can be my critic"

"Would you mind if I come along?"

"Good, then I will have two critics?"

"What about three?" Looking over at Troy as he spoke. Ruthie really did not want him to come, but what could she say? Well, the more the merrier. When you see the rehearsal, I want you all to be honest with me, but not too hard on me because I haven't danced much in years. However, we want the program to be a success."

Ruthie had a group of twenty girls and boys she was training in a dance routine as part of the entertainment for the Youth Convention. Carrie was not surprised at Ruthie's dancing ability because she had gone with Ruthie on campus when she worked with others, putting on a show, before she got involved with Troy. Troy had never seen her because he never hung around for the college social programs

Mrs. Thompson and Troy were amazed with Ruthie's dancing and singing abilities.

"Mom, I never knew she was so talented, did you?"

"No, Troy, I didn't know she could sing that well. I have heard her mess around with Carrie and Susan at the house but her singing never sounded like much or maybe I wasn't expecting much. I suppose it was there all the time." Carrie spoke up.

"I did, you should hear her sing some of Whitney Huston's hit songs. I'll go tell her to sing one of them for you. She will."

"No Honey, we can't bother her."

"Mom, let me go. Besides, I want to hear her." Before Mrs. Thompson could say another word or attempt to answer, Carrie was on the stage standing beside Ruthie." Just about that time Ruthie ran into a problem with some of the youth who started to complain about first one thing and then another. She took a few minutes to compare her life with theirs

As she began to speak to them, it seemed like all ears were listening.

"Look, most of you are quite fortunate. You have parents who love you. My parents did not want me. They did everything they could to get rid of me and by the time I was nine, I was placed in a shelter for unwanted and incorrigible children." She went on to tell the kids about the Carters, her first real home and what happened to them.

Ruthie and the others had problems with the same few children at other rehearsals and she knew if they had not straightened up this time, they would be out of the show. She had discussed minor issues about her life with Carrie and Susan before when they had a disagreement with their parents. She wanted them to know how important parents are and what they expect from them as children. Her life problems help to bring them back in line.

Everyone in the Hall could hear what Ruthie was saying because of the tone of her voice and the number of youth she was trying to get the message through to.

Troy had begun to understand why Ruthie was so determined to avoid certain things. He felt a lot of love and respect for her. He knew he had to have her back, even if he had to wait for all of her love.

After Ruthie got everyone in line, she took Carrie's hand and led her back to her seat, sat down beside her and watched the performance of the group.

"Carrie, I will sing that song for you, as soon as they finish their part, okay?

"Mrs. Thompson what do you think, so far. I have to get tough with them sometimes because the same ones are always complaining. These children do not have a lot of problems and what few they do have are of their own makings. They tend to act before they think, run before they walk and try to see a problem before they get there. There are so many great things they can do in, and with their lives, if they only give life a chance. So many are ruining their lives with drugs, crimes and having babies to care for when they cannot care for themselves. They have so many more wonderful things they can do and life needs them to do things."

"Ruthie, that was a clever idea you had telling them a story like that. Maybe they will believe it." Before Ruthie could respond, Carrie butted in.

"Mother, didn't you know all the horrible things that Ruthie went through? That was no story, that was the truth. Every time we were not good, she would tell me and Susan how wonderful you and Dad are and how much you all loved us. You remember when Susan was so angry with you last month, she was going to run away. I called Ruthie and she left work to meet her. I bet you didn't know that."

"Carrie."

"Oh Mommy, please don't tell Susan, Please?"

Troy was listening to everything being said and He was watching every move Ruthie made. He didn't want to believe what he was hearing.

"Ruthie, how could a beautiful girl like you endure so many atrocities?"

"I had no choice, however, there are some good people in the world which makes it all worthwhile. Just think, if I had a normal childhood, I would not have met Carrie." Upon hearing that Carrie gave Ruthie a tight squeeze. Troy raised his head and spoke with a note-of sadness in his voice. "Can I squeeze you like that?"

"Well, yes, you, Susan.... looking over at Mrs. Thompson, and you mother. Ruthie got up." Went back to work."

She sang Whitney Houston's first hit song.

Troy's friend Delia was trying to get closer to him, but he never thought of her as someone he wanted to marry. She was just someone he hung out with and tried to make Ruthie jealous. She was never a girlfriend. The closest they ever got was when he take her out to dinner sometime. He thought his parents liked her and his sisters because she would sit down with them and show his sisters how to use makeup and discuss the latest fashions that young girls like. Delia was a fashion expert and worked for one of the best designers in the area.

I might add, Delia was having some serious problems. She wanted to get married and was spreading rumors that her and Troy would be soon. Troy had no intentions of marrying her because he wanted Ruthie. He probably knew Ruthie's routine on a day-to-day basis better than she did.

Troy's family had developed a gross dislike for Delia for some good reasons. She wanted the social status that went along with Troy's job as well as the money. She pitied Carrie and tried to tell Susan that she should be thankful that the same thing had not happened to her. Mrs. Thompson had heard enough of Delia's sarcastic comments because it was driving Carrie into hysteria. Carrie needed more love, not criticism, she needed understanding, not put-downs, she didn't need to be reminded of her problems, she needed to forget and go on with her life. Just watching Ruthie now, Mrs. Thompson realized how much of a friend she really was, especially to her daughters,

After the practice was over they wanted to follow Ruthie home. She tried to discourage, but they insisted. Ruthie invited them in for a few minutes. Her apartment was a little larger than the one at the Thompsons. She had purchased more furniture, which set her back financially(they thought) from the looks of it, thought Mrs. Thompson.

"Ruthie, this is nice."

"Thanks, Mrs. Thompson. It's home for now."

"Mom, can I spend the night with Ruthie? Troy can pick me up in the morning and drop me off to the summer school activities?"

"No, not tonight. Why don't you wait and do a little planning. Don't you realize Ruthie has a life away from you?"

"Okay Mom. Ruthie, when can I spend the night?"

"Carrie, let me finish getting my thoughts organized for the convention then I will plan for us to do some things, However, as for spending the night anytime your Mom says, is alright with me. I don't go anywhere. I am usually home by six or seven when I am working. Right now I attend one class a week on Tuesdays.."

Troy didn't want Carrie to stay tonight because he wanted to come back and talk.

"Carrie, not tonight because I want to talk to Ruthie about a few things later, if she doesn't mind. Looking toward Ruthie as he spoke. "Okay, Ruthie?" She didn't want to deny him in front of Carrie, she just said "Yes, I suppose." Troy felt a little relieved.

"I'll be back as soon as I take them home." After they left Ruthie started her dinner. Before too long, Troy was back. He came in and stretched out on the couch. Troy had to figure out a way to start the conversation.

"Are you preparing dinner for me too, Baby?"

"You are welcome to dinner, but let's get one thing straight 'I am not your BABY any more remember, now what is it you want to talk to me about?"

"Us, and it can wait until after dinner."

"Us, what about us?"

"I said, it can wait until after dinner." Troy got up, walked over to Ruthie, kissed her on the cheeks before she could say don't and went into her bedroom. He said "Wake me up when dinner is ready." And closed the door. Ruthie mumbled to herself. "I don;t believe what I am seeing. This man is 'nuts'. She went back to her cooking. After about an hour dinner was ready. She went to the bedroom door and called Troy. He rolled over facing her.

"Come here Baby, please."

"I don't mess around with other women's men and you had better come on if you want to eat."

"I only belong to one woman and that's you. Let's get married this week?"

"Troy."

"Baby, I am serious. I love you," He could feel the hostility welling up in Ruthie.

"Troy."

"Okay, I am coming to dinner." She pointed him toward the bathroom.

"You can wash up, if you like. The bathroom is right through there."

"Baby, I will be here every night at six thirty for dinner."

"No you won't either. You may be at Delia's house."

"Look, it's nothing between me and that woman. I was just angry because you teased me so much."

"I never teased you."

"You mean every time you put your arms around me, you got real close to me, told me you loved me, you really meant it?"

"Troy, sit down and stop asking stupid questions." Troy stopped teasing Ruthie and got serious. He talked about his future plans. He was looking around for a house and he wanted her to help him make the decision about his selection.

"I want you to select the home that you will be sharing with me, "

To Ruthie, he was down right ridiculous. To Troy, he was serious and meant every word he said.

After that night, Troy came by every night for dinner. Ruthie tried to discourage him, She told him she was no longer considering marriage and that her plans to become a Doctor were imminent but Troy did not adhere to anything she said. He continued to pop-in wherever she went. He would come over to her apartment just when dinner was ready. He talked about future plans which included her. Nothing she said discouraged him. He would pick her up from work and take her any place she wanted to go. Ruthie tried to avoid him. It seemed he would outguess her every time. If she left work early and went a different way, the next thing she knew he was pulling up alongside her. He was being so nice and she did not want to be rude, so she just played along. Ruthie liked Troy a lot and did not want to lead him on.

"Troy, look I don't want to just lead you on, I want you to know I am serious about Med School and do not plan to consider marriage until I am done, Please don't include me in your plans."

"Look Ruthie, I am in love with you and want you to be my wife and I am willing to wait until you are ready. If our relationship has to be boyfriend, girlfriend, then I will settle for that. I am no longer house hunting. I have decided to buy some land to build our house. It's going to take a while, probably a few years. When we get married I don't plan to have any children for at least two years and I don't want us to have a mortgage. My plans are to have everything paid off when we move in because I want ten children. Any mortgage money will be a saving for our children education." '

"You want ten children?" Ruthie laughed.

"Sure, what's wrong with that?" I want you to help me design the home you would like to live in. I think we should have at least five bedrooms. What do you think?"

"Well, with ten children, I suppose so."

All Ruthie could envision at this point was to see herself pregnant every year and all her dreams will never materialize.

After all she went through in life, she did not want to give in. Yes, she felt like she was in love with Troy but is he expecting too much of her? Will he expect her to change to benefit him? Will he become angry if she chooses to deviate away from his expectations? Would he deny what she wanted her way to go and the accomplishments she wanted to pursue? Ruthie knew what she wanted and the way she wanted to go. Can Troy fit in? She knew she was determined to be Ruthie and would not allow anyone or anything to change her mind. Life for her was not to be all about the way someone else wanted it to be.

Troy tried to understand her expectations. He tried to mellow his demands when talking about their life together. He talked about what he would like and the things he foresees.

He would tell Ruthie how much he loved her. Ruthie tried to shy away from his hugs and kisses, but he would not let her get away from that. Whenever he got ready to leave, she would walk him to the door so she could lock it behind him and just when she got ready to close the door he pulled her in his arms. She told him "I love you because you are impossible."

Those words were uplifting to Troy, it helped to know that Ruthie was in love with him. He knew that there was still hope and he was not fighting a losing battle. There were times he had to go away for his job, he would always call her, even if it was just to talk about what they did that day and when he came home, Ruthie's place was his first stop. There were times he would be waiting at her door steps when she came home. Since she had agreed to be his girlfriend they would go out to dinner, movies, and the theater on long drives together but never overnight with him. Troy truly loved Ruthie and he learned to respect Ruthie's decisions whatever they may be. Sure, there were many other girls who had their eyes on him but his eyes were only for Ruthie. To know Ruthie, was to love her, because she was honest, kind, loving, truthful and she doesn't try to do anything that will cause a person harm. When Bob Brene tried to force himself on her she tried not to hurt him and she didn't allow anyone to pressure her to file charges on him. What was important to her was that she managed to get away without being harmed. Also with Mr Crossley, she could have told his wife about his advances but she did not want to cause a break up in him and his wife's relationship. Ruthie is all about love even when it affects her at times. She tries her best to show her love but never to expect anything in return. She knew when to let go and put a stop to expecting a response from others. She never fights for love and respect but allows it to go the distance and steps back. Throughout her life Ruthie demonstrated an exemplary pattern for her life. Her life showed that love is the example that we should follow and it is not necessary to demonstrate hate. We as human beings can accomplish anything we choose but must understand that rarely our desires do not materialize overnight or next week. Sometimes it takes years. We must stand our grounds, stay faithful to our desires and work on them daily.

Getting angry because others or in agreement with our beliefs will not help anyone. In life there are people with many types of goals different from one another. Many of their goals are based on their 'frame-of reference', 'family traditions and the kind of training in their homes'. As individuals we must determine what we want out of our lives and we must work on those goals continuously. We must also understand that others may see things differently from ours and try to change us the way they want us to be, to satisfy their desires. Many will try to use their 'frame of reference of love' to advocate their love, but when it affects a change in your goals for life, you must ask yourself, "What's love got to do with it?" One thing we must realize is that is a 'Supreme Being', most people know HIM as GOD, should be our first love. Then we must understand that we must love ourselves and stick to our goals and never allow others to make changes in our plans until we can see our future through them.

Ruthie thought much about her plans for Medical school. She had begun to see her life with Troy. She became very much in love with him but was doing her best to hide it. She thought much about medical school and after accomplishing those goals then what? She thought about a husband, children, being a wife and mother. "But ten children?" She thought a lot about children and the kind of mother she would be. She thought about how much love she would give them and they would never suffer. She believed Troy would be a good father because she saw how loving he was to his sisters and how obedient he was to his parents.

She had determined after a very restless night, the next time he asked her to marry him, she was going to say yes.

One evening she left work much earlier than usual to attend a community meeting. Midway into the meeting, Troy walked in. She could not imagine how he found the place because she never let on the night before that she was going anywhere.

When she saw him come in she realized she was glad he was there. She knew this night she would allow him to kiss her goodnight without a fight and if he asked her to marry him, she would say yes. After the meeting, she walked over to him.

"Are you looking for someone, Sir?"

"Uh huh."

"Who might that be? Maybe I can help you find her."

"What makes you think, it's a her?"

"Instinct, my Dear Sir, Instinct."

"Thanks, anyway, I have already found her."

Troy put his arms around Ruthie and kissed her on her forehead. "Are you ready to leave?"

"Yes"

"Have you had dinner?"

"Nope."

"Then, let's eat out tonight."

"That sounds great, "

After dinner Troy took Ruthie by his house, he told her Carrie wanted to show her something and let his family know they were still on good terms. Troy had not been saying much to his parents about Ruthie because knowing his mother she probably would have said 'why don't you get a girl that will do what you want her to do'? But Troy knew who he wanted. With the pressure he was applying he knew eventually Ruthie would be back in his arms and by taking her to his family, they would think they were closer. This would encourage Ruthie's decision to be like they were before and this time set a wedding date. Troy's parents were happy to see them together, especially Carrie and Susan.

When Troy went into the house, he went straight up to his room. After a few minutes he asked Carrie to tell Ruthie to come up and he needed some help with something. No sooner than Ruthie walked in the door, he pulled her in his arms and closed the door. Ruthie looked up at Troy with tears in her eyes. He took her in his arms and placed them on his shoulders and then slid his arms around her waist. Ruthie tightens her arms around his neck. Troy murmured three words. "Baby marry me." Ruthie looked up at him and said "Yes." Troy took Ruthie's hand and they walked down the stairs.

CHAPTER 14

"Mom, Why are you staring at me? Is something wrong?"
"I am sorry son, I was thinking how much you resemble your father."

"Mom, you are not supposed to be thinking about another man. Remember you are supposed to be marrying another man tomorrow. Are you having second thoughts."

"I can't help but think how much in love, your father and I were, when we got married"

"Aren't you in love with Todd?"

"I like him a lot, I guess I am, but not like your dad and I were, when we got married. Maybe it's because we are older and we both were married before."

"Mom, are you still in love with Dad?" Before Ruthie could answer the telephone rang.

Carrie called to tell them that Mrs. Thompson was in the hospital, she had a heart attack.

"Stay right there, we're on our way." Troy Jr looked over at his Mom. "What happened Mom?" "Grandma is in the hospital and they think it's a heart attack, Carrie is there now."

"Is Dad there?"

"I didn't ask, but I hope so."

"Oh!"

"Okay, Junior, I believe you want me to put you over my knees."

"Mother, I won't fit and besides you have not answered my question, I asked before the phone call. I have no alternative but to assume my own answer to that question."

Now, all the children were waiting for an answer to T. J's question. Ruthie's response was "We better get to the hospital."

Most of the children knew what was on their Dad's mind and also for the last couple days Todd said some strange things. "I hope your mother doesn't change her mind, if she does, I will understand."

That was why Amber was so quiet, because of the big change in Todd. A couple of weeks before, he couldn't wait to get married. They knew Todd loved their mother very much. Now when he spoke, he appeared to have a defeatist attitude, in reference to their plans.

When Troy found out Ruthie was seeing Todd, he went to him and told him to stay away because he would not allow any man to have his wife. When Todd found out that Troy had been going through the A. A program, he became a little frightened and tried to get Ruthie to elope. He wanted to marry her right away. Ruthie being Ruthie wanted to make sure she was doing the right thing. She and Troy had been divorced for about a year and semi- separated for about six month. For about six month Troy spent many nights with Ruthie, even though they were separated. For about a year neither of them saw anyone else. Troy had reverted back to a Momma's Boy. Even after the divorce he felt that Ruthie was still his wife and the divorce meant nothing. He felt that when he was home with the family, it was where he was supposed to be. Ruthie brought him back to reality. She stopped allowing him to sleep with her when he felt like it although she still loved him. She had to make Troy develop some meaningful priorities, either he was going to be his wife and they were going to be a family again or he was just going to be the children's father and visit them from time to time, but not her, unless it had something to do with the children.

CHAPTER 15

R uthie worked at the hospital and she taught at the college. She met Todd shortly after his wife died and just about the time Troy started having problems. Sometimes her and Todd would have lunch together, nothing demanding, just a normal lunch. They talked about their children and other things in general. When Todd found out she was getting a divorce, he asked her out a number of times, but she refused. About six months ago he took her to a movie and from that it led to other dates.

When Ruthie and Todd's relationship became somewhat serious and Troy found out about it, he could not take it. He began watching and visiting more often. He decided at that moment he would let no one take his wife and he went to see Todd. At that point he began to realize he was about to lose his wife of twenty years, who had given him nothing but love along with six loving children. He thought of what a fool he had been and this gave him the determination to get his act together.

Because of the A. A meetings, counseling and the additional duties on his job, he did not have time to sit down and talk to Ruthie. He had to reprove himself there and in between work on his alcohol problem as well as look after his mother and father, who was ill. Also he had to make sure too much was not left for Carrie to do. His counseling section helped him to realize that his parents' dependability on him to do everything for them caused him to use alcohol to ward off some of the demands made by his parents. This caused a problem in his marriage. Carrie wasn't much help, Susan was married and moved away. She had two small children and could not help. Ruthie worked and there were their six children. Ruthie would help from time to time and he limited that, she had enough to do. Still she would take it upon herself one afternoon a week and do their laundry. His parents could afford some outside help but refused. Troy realized he wanted his wife back and he wanted to live at home again and this time forever. If there is going to be a wedding, it's going to be with him and Ruthie.

Ruthie and Todd had planned to be married at another time much later, but Todd encouraged her to get married three month sooner.

T. J. and Amber knew what their father's plans were. He had asked them not to say a word to the other children and definitely not to their mother.

CHAPTER 16

On the way to the hospital, Ruthie thought about when Troy demanded that she marry him right away. When she said yes, that was the 'key factor'. When? he knew that would be his decision. Ruthie's thoughts were in about a year. When they walked into where his family were he announced, "Mom, Dad, Carrie, Susan, Ruthie and I are going to get married". They all, (with a question mark) were happy for them. When Troy took Ruthie home, he smothered her with kisses. Between kisses he spoke outright, not giving her a chance to respond. "Baby we will be getting married as soon as we get our licenses, understand?" And I don't want any objections." Each time she tried to respond he covered her lips with kisses. He tried his best not to go home that night but with all the pressure he put forth, all he got was a goodnight kiss.

"Baby the only thing I will understand tonight, is that you will agree to everything I say tonight, as I have with you. I am going home, but I don't want to. I love you and am abiding by your wishes."

"Troy, let's talk."

"No, you heard what I said."

"Honey, I do love you, but there is something I will not do until we are married."

"Okay but in my arms I am going to hold you for one hour and you will not fight me, understand?"

"Yes" He held her on the couch. As soon as Troy fell asleep, Ruthie got up, closed her bedroom door and went to sleep. When she woke up the following morning, Troy was standing over her. She looked up at him apologetically. "I am sorry Honey, but I just couldn't." Lifting her up in his arms. "At least I know you have feelings. I wasn't asleep when you got up, I thought it best that I let you go, "

"Honey, let's talk about our wedding plans."

"What is there to talk about?"

"I want to have a small church wedding and invite a few family and friends, okay?"

"How much time are you talking about?"

"Two or three month."

"Uh, did you say, two or three weeks?"

"Troy, please."

"Okay. six weeks, the most and if all plans are not in place, we will get married by whatever legal means, okay?"

"One more thing, we are going to apply for our licenses today and any other test required. I will make the arrangements and call you later. No class today, okay?"

"I have a final exam today at ten thirty and done by twelve."

"Okay, then I will pick you up about ten after twelve."

"That's okay I will drive and meet you here."

"I said, I will pick you up and I will be here to drop you off, as well. I am going to run home, take a shower and get a bite to eat.

Ruthie didn't know how she was going to get all the things that had to be done in thirty days.

She had the Youth convention, her job, time for Troy, planning the wedding, sending out invitations, the reception, her dress she wants to make and exams at college then she will begin to pull all this other stuff together. She thought, let me not forget the Church and the Minister.

Ruthie took a shower, got a bowl of cold cereal and settled down to review her notes and book for the final exam. No sooner than she sat down the telephone rang.

"Hello."

"Hi, Baby, I miss you."

"I miss you too. Are you still at home?"

"Yes and on my way out the door. Honey, mother wants to talk to you. See you at ten to drop you off at college. Bye honey. I love you."

"Ruthie Troy told me the good news, is there anything I can help you with?"

"Oh Mrs. Thompson, do you mean that? I don't know where to begin. It's going to be small because I only have thirty days or else we elope, those are my orders. I suppose the main thing is the Church, Preacher, a place for the reception, caterer and the invitation out. If you can do any of those things, I would appreciate it. I have finals today and after that I can think. Oh, by the way, do you think Carrie and Susan would like to be in the wedding? I also have one other friend I am going to ask."

"If they were not a part of the wedding, I don't think I would be able to live with them. I will have as much information as possible about the other things tonight. Call me are, come by my house tonight."

Troy picked Ruthie up on time, they went and registered for their marriage license and made an appointment for their blood test later that afternoon. They went back to the apartment to discuss their future plans and came to an agreement.

Ruthie would finish college and work for a year. They agree not to start a family for at least two years. Ruthie money would help purchase the furniture for their home. Also Troy's would purchase their home because they did not want a mortgage. He already had quite a bit of money saved. He was earning $80. 000 a year on his job, living with his parents, and spending very little. Even when he was in college and working part time his lifestyle was still the same. His parents always had a livable income and never had to lean on him. Ruthie still had about $75. 000 in the bank from the Carters because she spent very little for college. She always received a lot of scholarships because she got good grades in college. Her largest bill was her rent and she worked and earned enough to pay what was due, feed and dress herself and had close to half her salary to save. Troy decided to purchase the land and design and build the home the way he wanted. He wanted a lot of children. So the agreement was 'no mortgage and no furniture bills'. Ruthie suggested moving in with his parents.

"Honey we could save more if we move in with your parents, I wouldn't mind."

"No, that is out of the question." Troy didn't want to live with his parents because he felt it would be too much interruptions, he wanted Ruthie all to himself. He knew how attached Carrie was to Ruthie and it would be impossible to have the privacy he wanted. Troy shared with Ruthie all of his desires for the future, he talked about his job and what is expectedof him there. Ruthie was included, in some way, in everything he had planned.

"Honey, there will be times I will be required to attend business conventions cross country and I want you with me, so I am telling you now, no matter what job or class you are taking, when I go, you go. I have no intention of ever leaving you alone overnight."

"Troy, I am not afraid to be alone."

"That is not the point, You are not listening, I said you will not be left alone by me overnight. Just always be prepared to come with me.

CHAPTER 17

•••••••••••••••••••••••••••••

Ruthie called her father and he agreed to come to the wedding along with his wife, Gloria. All her sisters and brothers, Mrs. Leys, Doctor and Mrs. Connors, the Crossley's, Marlo, Mrs. Velez, her counselor from the high school and a few other acquaintances she met over the years. Troy had several friends and many family members who would be attending the wedding and reception. What started out as a small wedding of about one hundred people and a wedding party of five turned into a reception of about five hundred and a wedding party of twelve.

Carrie would be the Maid of Honor, a friend of Ruthie's from work would be the Matron of Honor and her sisters and some of Troy's relatives and Ruthie's brothers and sisters would make up the rest of the party. Most of all her relatives would play some part in her wedding.

All of her family came a day before the wedding. She had to reserve a few hotel rooms for them because her apartment was not large enough to accommodate all of them. Ruthie was very happy because everyone was making such a fuss over her. She had always made a special effort to keep in touch with her family and keep them abreast of what was happening in her life, school and work. Many times they have called her for financial favors and she reached out and helped them. She never let them know anything about what the Carters had done for her. On special holidays she would always remember them with nice gifts and sometimes money when she was unsure what they needed or wanted. Ruthie would visit from time to time for short visits, because she never felt welcome. They never ask her to stay overnight. She loved her family but did not feel loved or truly accepted. They were the only family she knew she had.

She felt that she could truly love them regardless of how they feel about her. She was invited to a few parties, she went but did not stay very long because of what was going on.

Ruthie's father and his wife stayed at her apartment, along with a few of the children and the rest at the hotel. Troy knew most of them because he had taken her over to visit a few times.

Ruthie's two brothers and a few of Troy's friends took him out on the town the night before the wedding and then to a Bachelor's Party. Ruthie stayed home putting the finishing touch on her wedding dress. She knew she had to be alert because all the girls would be at her place the next morning preparing for the wedding. The wedding was scheduled for one o'clock.

Troy was the first person at the church, along with his Dad. (an hour before to be exact) His father had to take his car keys because he wanted to go and pick Ruthie up.

"Troy, look, we are an hour early."

"Dad, she should be here, she is never late."

"Troy she is not late. All the ladies will be coming at the same time, just relax."

"Dad, she should still be here, all she had to do was put on her dress."

"Sometimes it takes woman a little longer, to just put on a dress"

"I'm going to call to see if everything is alright. Dad, suppose she changes her mind, then what am I supposed to do? Dad give me the keys, I'll be right back." Mr. Thompson was so happy when Ray, Troy's best man came in. Ray started feeding him information which helped to distract his attention, for a while.

"Troy, I have everything finalized for you…………….. he went on to emphasize the name of the hotel, plane tickets, time flight leaves, luggage, change of clothing after the reception, time they will be picked up to catch their flight etc. Before Ray was quite finished, someone shouted, "she's here". Troy stood up, Ray sat him back down.

"Hey, hold on there, where do you think you are going? They are not ready for you yet."

"Come on man, I want to see my Baby."

"Look man, you will begin a lifetime together in less than a half hour."

Finally, Troy received his cue to walk in. It seemed like the whole city was coming in before his bride. Everything seems to be taking so long. Then the music changed to(Here comes the bride) Then he began to breathe more easily. Before too long the minister said," I now pronounce you Husband and Wife, you may salute the bride". Troy kissed her with all the feelings a person can have for another. He whispered in her ear, "Nothing can save you now, you belong to me forever." After the ceremony they took a few pictures and stopped a few places and took some more pictures, then headed for the reception hall. At the reception more pictures were taken. Then Troy said no more pictures.

No sooner than they cut the cake, Troy was ready to leave. Ruthie tried to ask her sister a little about the first time with a man but Troy would not let her get one step away from him. He did allow her to dance two seconds with her dad, but nobody else. She wanted to talk to some of her married friends but she was so busy and did not have the time. She was too embarrassed to say anything to Mrs. Thompson. She knew how she felt in Troy's arms. She tried to get away to question her sister but it didn't happen.

"Troy I'll be right back, I want to talk to Lana for a few minutes, Okay Honey?"

"No, because I want to dance with you right now, you can talk to her when we return from our honeymoon. I'll take you over to visit."

"But Honey, what I have to ask her will not take long." Troy took Ruthie by the hand and led her to the dance floor. They stayed at the reception for as short a time as they could.

Troy wanted to get Ruthie out of that dress, he wanted their honeymoon to start at Ruthie's apartment before they leave. Everything was at Ruthie's apartment, so that was where they went to change their clothing. The limousine took them there and Ray followed, he made sure they had everything they needed and then left, also giving them a time they would be picked up and taken to the airport. After Ray left Troy locked all the doors. Ruthie soon realized she had no more excuses to protect her.

Ruthie was anxious to get back to the reception for a few minutes and thank everyone individually for their participation and help and still get to the airport on time. She did not believe they had time for anything else but Troy had plans established which she did not know about.

"Honey, unzip my dress please." Troy had most of his clothing off. He unzipped Ruthie's dress (gown) and helped her out of it. He picked up the gown and laid it across the chair. At that moment, Ruthie knew she would not be going anywhere right away.

They had just enough time to stop by the reception and thank everyone and get to the airport on time.

Ruthie and Troy spent two glorious weeks together. They got to really know each other and enjoy their time together. They showered each other with love. Troy kept her all to himself. Most times they had their meals sent up to their room. Ruthie was happy, she felt she found her place in life which was with Troy. The first time in her life she realized that she was truly in love with someone and there could never be another one she could love as much.

When Troy and Ruthie returned from their honeymoon, they were home three day before he would allow Ruthie to call anyone to let them know they were home nor did they answer the telephone. Ruthie thought that they should at least let his parents know they were home.

"Honey, don't you think we should let your parents know that we are home because they may be worried?"

"Why should they worry, we are adults?"

"Honey, being adults, has nothing to do with it."

"Then why bother?"

"Ho.. ney"

"Okay, call them. Call my parents but do not invite them over nor accept an invitation from them, because I am not ready to share you with anyone." Ruthie walked over and dial their number and handed the telephone to Troy. Troy took the telephone, pushed the receiver down and put the telephone on the table and took Ruthie in his arms." I will call them later, right now I want to hold my wife in my arms, would that be alright with you Mrs. Troy Delan Thompson?"

Troy and Ruthie shared a great amount of love for each other from the time they were married. Arguments were non- existent. If a concern came up, one or the other would compromise.

While Ruthie was working on her Bachelor's Degree, Troy was working on his Doctor's Degree.

Ruthie had to change some of her classes around so they could be at the college at the same time. She did as many as she could and he was pleased. They were able to study together and since she had more time then he did, he would outline what he needed to type and she would do most of the typing. Many times she would do the necessary research and he would review it and then type it for him in his own words.

Troy was able to complete his Doctor's Degree one year after Ruthie received her Master's Degree. They were able to move into their home two years after they were married.

Three month after they moved, Ruthie became pregnant with her first child. Troy made her quit work, but he allowed her to work on her Doctor's Degree while sitting home doing nothing. If and when she showed any sign of fatigue he would make her stay home or drive her to class and pick her up. Ruthie was pretty smart so she carried as many classes as the college would allow.

CHAPTER 18

Their first child Troy Jr. was born close to three years after they were married. They called him T. J. About a year and a half later, Amber came along, then Lois, Larry, Gravina and then Thesa. Each child was about a year and a half apart. After Thesa, Ruthie felt that it was time to stop. Troy did not want to stop, he wanted ten children but Ruthie felt that it was time for her to stop and she did everything she could to prevent any more pregnancies. Troy questioned her and wondered why she had not become pregnant again. She never lied to him, just kept him wondering.

Troy started drinking, his parents were ill and constantly demanding his attention, Susan had married and moved out of state and Carrie had gotten married and moved within the city but not close to them. They didn't want to lean on her, so they placed all the pressure on Troy. Mrs. Thompson had blamed all of her problems on Ruthie. She felt that it was Ruthie's fault that Susan went out of State to college and Carrie got married and moved so far away from them.

She also felt that Ruthie kept Troy tied up with all those grands when whenever she needed him he was right there before they came along. Whenever Troy came over she would encourage him to stay and do whatever it took to keep him there.

Troy started drinking quite heavily and the least little thing upset him. He reached a point where he would go and spend the night at his parents home. They would uphold him in any thing he did. Even with that he still was not satisfied, he dranked even more. Sometimes he would stay away for days at a time and Mrs. Thompson did not have the courtesy to call to let Ruthie know he was alright and at their home. Most times she found out by Carrie. Troy would be there but when he began to miss Ruthie and the children he would come home. Ruthie loved Troy very much and she did everything she knew to please him.

She even gave up the idea of not having any more children. She did nothing to prevent her from becoming pregnant.

She kept herself, their home neat and clean, the children neat and she never wasted money.

Every once in a while Troy would have these expensive dinner parties, she dealt with that. Food and liquor galore. Nothing cheap, always the top of the line stuff. If she said anything negative, he would get upset and accuse her of not loving him anymore. He made a good salary but with six children, money should not be wasted ridiculously and Troy was wasting too much. On one of his extended stays at his parents, Ruthie decided to return to work.

Throughout their lives, Carrie had remained her fast friend. She could always discuss most anything with her. Carrie had gotten very upset with her parents for allowing Troy to hang around their home drinking. Troy would stay sober enough to hold onto his job, but not his family.

Ruthie tried to explain to the children, but it was kind of hard. She was not sure she was getting the right things through to them. She never said anything negative about Troy to them. She tried to make them understand that all people have problems from time to time, even adults. She wasn't sure what went wrong between her and Troy. In fact, she did not know at all, but knew she had to sit them down and talk to them and hear what they were going through or had any questions she would try to answer.

"I would like to talk to all of you tonight, does anyone have a problem being home by six? Okay, good. If you have any question about anything, bring them up tonight and I will do the best I can to answer them.

T. J. felt that he should be the one to ask questions because he was the oldest, but he had a good idea why their mother wanted to talk to them. He dreads the day his parents would tell them that they would no longer be living together. He knew his father had not been around too often and he knew about his drinking problem. He knew also that his mother suddenly went back to work and it had to be for a good reason for all of these things to be happening. T. J saw the break-up of some of his friends' parents and many horrible things that went down in their separation. He wondered what would happen with his parents. So far, it seems as if none of the things that have been happening in their home have happened in his friends home, it's just that his father drinks a lot and stays over his grandma's. Why? He did not know. He knew one thing, his mother cries a lot and when his father comes home they seem very happy. T. J. knew another thing, for sure, his mother never drinks alcohol, nor did she have any outside relationship with another man, he checked that out to make sure and he can say the same for his father. His father only drank and stayed over with his grandparents. He could not understand why they had not made him come home. His parents did not allow them to hang around anybody's home, not even their grandparents. Didn't they realize that they wanted and needed him at home. Amber thoughts were much the same as T. J. 's. She would go by their grandparents home almost everyday to see their father. Sometimes he was too drunk to realize she was there. She had reached a point where she would go to her grandparents home, greet them and go directly to her father's room and if he was asleep, she would bid them goodbye and leave. Ruthie would always know when she went over because would always tell her what happened. Amber began to notice when she told her mother about her dad, she would leave the room and when she returned her eyes were a bit red and puffy, because she had been crying. Amber understood that she tried to hide it but she knew. She was sort of glad they were going to have the family discussion, because she needed some answers. Lois was a bit different, she was angry with her father, she saw no need for the way he kept leaving and coming back upsetting their mother. She was really going to let him have it. She felt the drinking was just a 'cop- out' She did not go along with that illness bit. You drink, eat too much, smoke because you want to. She felt that if you really love and care for someone and what you are doing is hurting that person, if you really want to, you should stop. Lois remembered at one time her marks in school was not that great, but when her parents sat down and spoke to her about them and told her how much they loved her and wanted the best for her, she brought her grades up because she knew she was loved and she loved her parents very much and did not want to disappoint them. Larry and Gravina were at an age where not too many things bothered them as long as their parents were in reach, which they were, in a way. They were active in school and had other outside activities. Their day consisted of who would drop them off and pick them up from wherever they had to be. Thesa was a daddy baby. Whenever he would come home he had to sit down with her and listen while she went over her life history with him. It was his solemn duty to tuck her in every night. When Troy stayed away too long, Ruthie, or, one of the other children, had to take her over to Troy at their grandmas.

When Ruthie tried to talk to Troy, he would accuse her of nagging and when she said nothing he said, she did not love him anymore. She loved him but did not want to be considered a nag so she felt that if he was unable to recognize the love she had for him she felt, 'what's the use of constantly repeating herself.

When she went back to work, he 'hit the ceiling'. "Honey, all the children are in school and I will only be working part time, for now. We can use the money because T. J. is in college and Amber will be soon."

"I can afford to send my children to college." Troys' salary was twice as much as it was when they got married.

The discussions became more frequent and Ruthie became more silent. She just kept working and putting her money away for the children's education, if needed. Troy kept fussing, and she just ignored whatever he had to say. Ruthie felt she continued her education for a reason and was not going to let it be wasted. Troy had to see some things her way.

Ruthie knew her mother-in-law had a lot to do with the way Troy was acting. She examined in her mind about a lot of the things Carrie had commented on and put them together and came up with the feeling that Mrs. Thompson was angry with her because Troy cared so much about her and their children. She for a long time noticed it, but did not want to make Troy realize how his mother really felt about her and the children. She was always kind and loving as well as respectful to her. Mrs. Thompson was never that loving and kind grandmother to their children. She expected Troy to seek her approval about where they were going to live and because he failed too she blamed everything on Ruthie. Regardless of all she felt about Ruthie, for Troy's sake, Ruthie kept those things to herself. She wondered when Troy was going to open his eyes and see his mother for who she really was and how he was neglecting his family. Troy was always there for her and he would change anything he planned to do and go to her aid, when she called. Mrs. Thompson questioned why they built their home when there were so many empty houses already built, why they were having so many children, it was always "Ruthie, why? why? And how do you expect my son to be able to put all these children through college?" She could never say "this is what Troy wants." That response would have started a big argument. So Ruthie would let her think what she wanted to.

She thought about when Troy quit their relationship that time when she would not allow him to sleep with her, Mrs. Thompson was angry with her and asked her to find another place to live.

That evening after dinner when everyone was settled, Ruthie had all the children gathered in the family room.

"I guess you all want to know what I am going to say, maybe some of you already know and have some idea about what I'm going to talk about. Well, if you have been thinking about your father and I, then you are right. I want you to know what happened between your father and me has no reflection on any of you. I still love your father very much and I don't know where I failed him or what started him to drink. Sometimes two people can live happily together for many years and something happens which will cause them to separate and in many cases get a divorce
. The way things are now, your Dad and I may have reached that point. As I said before, I still love him very much, but I don't feel that it is right to try holding onto him if there is someone else which will make him happy again as we were, at one time. I believe it is only right to let him go. I do not feel it will benefit him in any way if I continue to hold onto

him and he remains miserable because of it, it is better that he go where he will find the happiness he deserves. I have asked him to come home and I told him I love him very much. I also asked him what went wrong but he could not give me an answer either. You must understand these things happen and it has happened between your father and me. Maybe he fell out of love with me. I can't say but that is the way it seems. I can accept that and you must also. I know one thing for sure, your father loves all of you very much. I asked him to come tonight but knowing him as I do, I didn't think he would. Some men do not like to be penned down where they have to respond to questions asked by people they love. This house is always open to your father. If he wants to come visit or stay with you he can and he knows it. The only thing is we will not share the same bed. I feel I have to let him know that he is free to go and do what pleases him. I want you all to know and never forget, because your Dad and I loved each other so much, all of you children are here. No problem existed in our relationship until I told him, I thought we had had enough children. When I saw a problem with that, I changed, but it did not stop what I had already started. He might have gotten upset because no more babies were coming."

"Mom."

"Yes Lois."

"Did Grandma have anything to do with you and Dad breaking up?"

"I don't think so, I love your grandma very much and I think she loves me, in her own way."

"Think?"

"Did you say something T. J?"

"No, not really, I was only thinking out loud."

"Is it a thought you can share with us?"

"No, not really, not at this time anyway."

"Is there any problem or question anyone has I will try to answer."

"Mommy?"

"Yes Thesa."

"When will daddy be coming home to stay? I miss him."

"Honey, I don't know if he will come home to stay, but anytime you want to see him we can call him and someone will take you over to where he may be, okay?"

"Can I go over to grandma tomorrow and stay all night with Daddy?"

"Sure, but we must call daddy to see if he will be home. You know, sometimes he has to go away on business trips and that is a must for his job."

"Mommy Grandma said daddy is her big baby and she is glad he came back home. Mommy grandma is funny. I told her I am daddy's baby and I want him home and I would be glad if he comes home. Mommy I want daddy home, "sniff, sniff, sniff.""

"Thesa, honey, come here. You know what, you are going to spend the night in my room, in my bed and we are going to talk all night about why daddy is not here. Do you think you can stay awake while I explain?" A big smile came on Thesa's face because she liked getting in bed with her mother. When Troy was home she got to fall asleep in their bed often. In fact Troy did that with all the children, which is why the children felt so important in the family. They had so many special privileges that sat them apart from the others, yet made them closer to each other. Troy had time alone with each child. None of them suffered for the love of either parent.

"Mother."

"Yes Larry."

"Do you think Dad will be able to come with me to the game next week?"

"I would say, give him a call and find out. Never be afraid to ask either one of us questions. If he has to work or go out of town. If you will have me, I will come along, but I think he will take you. Let me know in time, because I will have to call Aunt Carrie. Did you want me to call daddy? I am not mad at him, don't forget that."

"Okay Mom, I will call him and let you know."

"Gravina, do you have any questions about anything?"

"No Mommy, not now, you explained everything so well that you answered any questions and concerns I had in mind before the discussions started."

"I want you all to come to me and go to your father any time if you have any questions about anything, anytime, understand? We are your parents and will always be and we love you regardless of what happens with us. Even if both of us remarry someone else, that will not stop us from being your parents. I thank you for loving me and I am proud to be one of your parents.

CHAPTER 19

••••••••••••••••••••••••••••

Carrie had gotten married and she and her husband lived not very far from Ruthie, so when Ruthie needed a sitter she was right there. Carrie couldn't have any children nor did her husband want any, so they enjoyed Ruthie and Troy's. Carrie's husband was a staff physician at a city hospital about thirty miles away. There were times when he worked long hours and instead of driving home for two or three hours to sleep he would remain at the hospital and take a nap. Carrie would stay with Ruthie and the children.

Ruthie went over to her mother-in-law's house as seldom as possible. Carrie loved her mother, but she also loved Ruthie as well, so she told her that her mother blamed her for a number of things. When she told her about what her mother said, Ruthie smiled, when she responded.

"Really, Oh no, it was not my idea. I am sorry she feels that way. Sometimes we are quick to judge others. I am sure she didn't think that. I had no say in those decisions." And she just let it go. There were other comments Carrie made about her mothers' feelings for Ruthie. Because Mrs. Thompson was Troy's mother, she said nothing. Her mother-in-law was angry with her because they did not move in with them after they were married but it was Troy's idea. She was angry because they did not purchase the house down the street from them. Ruthie liked it but Troy wanted to design and build the house he wanted. Blame her because Susan went to college out of state, but she tried to get her to attend the college she and Troy went to which was right down the street from where they lived, but Susan preferred not to. She wanted to get away from home. She said nothing to Troy about his mother and she tried to show her as much love as possible and she truly loved her. Ruthie felt that deep in her heart Mrs. Thompson loved her because she never did anything to harm and discredit her. She just did not want to believe her son would want to distance himself from her, so she had to blame someone else. Ruthie felt that she knew the truth and if she must take the blame, so be it.

Ruthie would have the children call their grandmother or she would take them over at least once a month, if they wanted to stay over she would not object unless it was a school the next day. The Thompsons were lonely and they wanted their children to make a fuss over them but they failed to realize that they had their own families and careers to think about. When Troy started to get upset about 'whatever' and started going over, they encouraged him to stay. He fell into their trap. Ruthie believes they welcome their divorce because they wanted their little boy home with them. After the divorce, Troy was home with Ruthie and the children often. Troy was spoiled, he didn't think the divorce meant very much. He felt that he had every right to his wife as he had before. When Ruthie started refusing his advances, he began to drink even more. He took leave from his job and when it was time to return he heard about Dr Todd Raine was interested in his wife

And was going to ask her out on a date. That information got back to him. At that point Troy began to take a good look at himself and wonder what had happened between him and his wife. He knew he could never allow any other man to have his wife. He began to assess his life and what he saw upset him quite a bit. Troy knew one thing, he had to stop drinking. It was hard in the beginning because his mother was constantly replenishing his liquor supplies for him once it got low. He got the guts one day to tell her not to bring anymore in the house.

T. J. and Amber came to inform their father that T. J. had met a girl and they were engaged. To Troy this brought back memories of when he and Ruthie got engaged and got married. It really shocked him when T. J. asked him.

"Dad, why did you stop loving Mother and start drinking so much?"

"Son, I have never stopped loving your mother, we just ran into some problems and one day grandma said, "You two just as well get a divorce." And I did.

"I notice you tend to do everything Grandma tells you."

"Why do you say that?"

"Grandma told us that Mother would not let you stay here after you two got married. Did she tell you to stay here? Are, asked you. She is mad at Mother for that. Grandma doesn't like Mommy. She is mad at her for not letting you buy the house down the street and a lot of other things, like Aunt Carrie moving close to you and Aunt Susan going to college away from home, that is why she doesn't get to see her much. Daddy, Grandma don't like Mommy but Mommy said she loves her. I don't understand, how can Mommy love someone who hates her? It seems like you hate Mommy because you left us and came here to stay. Daddy, I want my wife to be like our mother. Mommy never talks bad about Grandma or anybody. She always tells us that she still loves you even after the way you have been staying away. She didn't want a divorce but she did not feel it right to hold onto you when you no longer care about her.

Troy knew he had to get himself together because he was unaware of what his children were saying about his mother. Ruthie never mentions anything to him about his mother accusing her of all those things. Well, he thought "that would be Ruthie" Anyway, why would his mother want to cause problems between him and his wife and children?.. Nah, not his mother.. Well, not once did she "say straighten up Troy and go home to your family," in fact she would get upset when he talked about going home to his wife and children. Troy apologized to them for his behavior and told them he loved their mother and will do whatever to get her back. He told T. J. and Amber what he wanted to do and asked for their help. They agreed to help as much as possible, however T. J. was working, attending college full time and was engaged. Amber was attending college out of state but was home most weekends. Troy would ask Lois and he knows he would get a lot of flax, but he will seek her help as well. Now, he was beginning to realize what Carrie was trying to tell him all along, about their mother and he was too dumb to understand.

When Carrie's husband got killed in that car accident, she came home to stay for a while but she could not stand what was happening to her brother, at that time so she moved back into her home.

Carrie was happy for Ruthie when she started going out with Todd. She knew her brother and her parents had done her wrong. Even though she had a sneaky suspicion that Ruthie was still very much in love with Troy. She suffered while he allowed his parents and liquor to destroy him.

CHAPTER 20

· ·

When Ruthie and the children arrived at the hospital, Carrie was glad to see them. She hugged Ruthie as if she had not seen them for months.

"How is Mother?"

"Ah Ruthie, that ornery old lady will be alright, she just wanted to frighten us. The doctor is still with her."

"How is Dad taking it?"

"He is right there with her. You know Mother doesn't get too far away from him."

Troy walked over from out of nowhere and took Ruthie by her arm.

"Hi, can we talk?" T. J. Amber and Lois walked over and kissed their Dad.

"Look, you children keep Aunt Carrie company, I want to talk to my wife about coming home." Lois was always very outspoken. "Dad, there is one thing you have to be conscious of."

"And what's that?"

"This lady is getting married to someone else tomorrow."

"Not if I can help it." With that, Troy took Ruthie's arm and led her out the door, into the car and drove off. Ruthie didn't bother trying to pull away; she allowed herself to be hustled into her ex in-laws house. Troy did not stop until he reached his bedroom. "Troy, we didn't have to come in here to talk."

"It is where I wanted to come, alright?" Ruthie said nothing, she walked over to the window, looking out at the apartment where she lived so long ago thinking about the first time Troy kissed her up there and how much she was in love with him.

Troy walked over and turned her around and kissed her. "Ruthie, I love you and you are not going to marry anyone else but remarry me, understand?, I mean it."

"Troy, I am sorry, but you know Todd and I will be married tomorrow. I did not think you cared for me any longer and I was lonely."

"Did you hear what I said and Dr Craine knows very well that he cannot have you, you belong to me and I have no intentions of letting you go. I have left you alone too long already. I am going to start making it up to you right now. Ruthie couldn't help but to return his kisses. Troy was her first and only love.

"Baby, why didn't you tell me about my mother and the things she blamed on you?"

"Troy, I just didn't want to start any confusion, can you understand my reasoning?"

"No, I should spank you right here and now for not telling me the things she said.

"Troy, I love your parents and I know they mean well, it's just that they love their children so much that they do not want anyone else to have them or love them as much. Try to understand what I mean."

"Okay, I'll try, but I 'll not forgive them for the pain and suffering they caused in our lives.

Also, I want you to know I haven had anything to drink in months, You are the one who fulfills my needs, not alcohol. I love you and I will never leave you and my children again. Please forgive me for being such a

122

louse, please?" Ruthie was spilling tears all over Troy and he was steadily kissing her. After she got a hold on herself she said." Troy I think we better get back to the hospital." Reluctantly he said." Yes, I suppose we must and I am going to talk to my mother when she feels a little better. Will that be alright with you? I must clear up the things you have been blamed for all these years.

Ruthie saw and felt a great difference in Troy. He seems to take more control of his decision making. He said two things which puzzled her. He asks why she didn't tell him about his mother's accusations and that they should visit his mother so she would not blame her for keeping him away. She wondered, did he realize what went on and some of the things she was accused of? She knew the children asked questions. Well, she thought, she would find out soon enough.

"Mrs. Thompson wasn't very happy to see Ruthie, nor did she mind too much because Ruthie would be a help to her because of her knowledge and skills in nursing. When they walked in the room, she looked past Ruthie.

"Troy Dear, where have you been? I have been worried about you." Taking his hand and trying pulling him down on the bed to sit. Troy leaned over and kissed her on her cheek. Then he got up and put his arms around Ruthie. As she walked over toward her mother-in-law, guided by Troy, she spoke.

"How are you feeling Mom?"

"Well, I feel pretty good, I thought you and Dr. Craine would be married by now."

"Mother, do you think for one minute I would let another man marry my wife?

" I am afraid son, she is no longer your wife."

"Well mother, to me she has always been my wife, but legally she will be again in a few days. I have always felt she belongs to me, why do you think I never went out with any other women. Mom where is Dad?"

"He went to pick up some magazines."

You can chat with Ruthie, I'm going to talk with the Doctor, be right back."

Troy went out the door, down the hall toward the nurses station.

Mrs. Thompson questioned Ruthie in a very snotty tone of voice. "Where have you been Ruthie? You haven been over for about a month?"

"I was at home preparing for a wedding that would never be."

"Why did you lead Dr. Craine, on like that?"

"Mom. I did not lead him on, He knew how I felt and he knew how Troy felt. I suppose it is fair to say Todd knew more about what may or may not happen in relation to our wedding plans then I did. I did not know how Troy felt about me any longer and I was lonely. When Todd asked me to marry him, I told him how I felt about Troy. He was willing to gamble, so I accepted his proposal on that basis. When Troy was coming around often, I felt a slimmer hope of us getting back together, but when he stopped coming altogether, I thought it was hopeless to hope for reconciliation any more, even then I had never stopped loving him. You know there was no real basis for our divorce. He drank because he thought I had stopped loving him. I let him go because I thought it was what he wanted. Now enough about me. I am here to make sure you get the proper care. Has everything been alright? I will be popping in often to make sure. I hope the children haven't been barging in too often. Troy told them you needed lots of rest. Mom, would you and Dad think about staying with us when you get released from the hospital, for a while. You and Dad can have T. J. or Amber's room and Carrie can have any other room, because Lois is away at college. Please discuss it with Dad, I would love to have you."

"I don't understand you......how can you be so nice?" Before Mrs. Thompson could finish her conversation with Ruthie, Mr. Thompson came in.

"Hello Ruthie," directing his attention to Mrs. Thompson. "Dear, looks like we are going to lose our son again. This young lady has recaptured his heart." Turning to Ruthie Mr. Thompson spoked. "Ruthie, Troy told me what his intentions are. I never realized how much he cared about you." "Mother, brace yourself, because I believe we were wrong about a lot of things." Mrs. Thompson did not want to admit she was wrong about anything, however, she wanted to ask Ruthie why she was being so nice to her because she knew she could not like her, especially when she just told her how much she disliked her. She knew Ruthie must have known how she felt about her. Mrs. Thompson knew what she was doing when she prevented Troy from going home many nights. She bought liquor and poured it for and watched him drink it to get back at Ruthie for causing so many problems in her household. She knew her children would not have moved so far away from her had not Ruthie charmed them. Who did she think she was fooling? She knew her children and they loved her and wanted to be near her at all times. Mrs. Thompson was getting ready to let her have it when Mr. Thompson walked in. It was a good thing he walked in when he did because she would have looked and felt like a fool. He touched on the reason Troy and Ruthie did not move in with them, after they got married it was Troy who refused and not Ruthie. Later on in a family discussion Troy would tell the whole family the reason he did not want to move in his parents home and the reason he chose to design and build his own home. All those things were his choice not Ruthie's. Susan told her parents why she chose to go to college where she did and that Ruthie tried to get her to stay close to home. She was determined to get away from home, she had enough of her parents' domineering rules. She had to prove to herself that she was capable of making it on her own. At that time Carrie spoke up and let her parents know that Ruthie had nothing to do with where they purchased their home, it was her husband who made the decision concerning their home and where it would be. Mrs. Thompson just sat with her mouth glue shut. It is supposed that she should have been thinking how wrong she was about Ruthie and the minds of her children.

It is sad to think how wrong a person can be about another but yet do not have the guts to apologize. In life we must learn to love one another and not look for reasons to readily accuse others of anything we haven't seen them do and even with that our eyes can play tricks on us many times. We may think we see things one way and something entirely different happened.

If we can overlook the negative and dwell on the positive things in life, life will be a lot sweeter for all of us. There would be less hate and more love and concern for each other.

CHAPTER 21

Troy took Ruthie home to pick up the other three children. Larry, Gravina and Thesa were waiting at home for their father to come pick them up so they could visit their Grandma.

When they got home, Ruthie wanted Troy to take the children to visit their grandma while she did a little food shopping. She wanted to make a special dinner for the family and children who would be returning to college the next day and also Troy who will be sleeping in one of the children's rooms until they get married.

"Oh, no baby, we will drop the children off at the hospital and we will go shopping together….. like we used to, okay?"

"But Troy."

"No butts."

"I only wanted to spare you the frustrations."

"Sweetheart, I like that kind of frustrations." After dropping the children off, Troy headed for home. After he passed the Supermarket, Ruthie thought for a moment he had forgotten.

"Honey, shopping?"

"No."

"Yes." When Troy came to the traffic light he put his arms around Ruthie and pulled her as close as possible to him.

"What did I say?"

"But Honey I need to pick up a few things for dinner. Honey, we have the rest of forever together."

"You mean that?"

"Yes."

"Okay, shopping it is."

When Mrs. Thompson was discharged from the hospital, she along with Mr. Thompson came to live with Ruthie and Troy and the children. Carrie would stay over sometimes to help out and just be with the family. After about a month Mrs. Thompson, was much better and they moved back home.

Ruthie continued to work. Troy wanted her to quit but she convinced him that her paycheck was a necessity, especially when they had three children in college at one time and about the time one finished another will be starting. Troy made a good salary but there was a place for Ruthie's to fit in. He agreed to let her work full time for a year and maybe part time there after.

Troy felt so bad about what he had done and he wanted to make it up to her. He wanted Ruthie close by him at all times. He did not like her teaching at the college because Todd lectured there often and he did not like her working at the hospital because Todd was on staff there. It took every nerve in Troy's body to allow her to be at the same place as Todd. Troy would find some oddball excuse to take Ruthie to work and pick her up for lunch. If she drove he would make sure she was where she was supposed to be at the time she was supposed to be there. Jealous he was of her and trusting, no. The only thing she was guilty of was loving him. Troy often thought about if he was in one of his drunken stupors and Ruthie had married Todd, he often thought, " what would he have done?" He does not feel he could ever forgive his mother for what she caused in their relationship. Ruthie was always kind and loving to his family, she never did anything to cause them harm. She helped Carrie believe in herself and gave Susan courage to move forward otherwise they would have been a sucker like he was. He almost lost the best thing that ever happened to him. Well he got her back now and that's what counts.

When Ruthie was not in her class, she had better be in her office. Troy knew to-the-minute how long it took her to get to and from her class. If she did not call him when she got back to her class he would call her with a barrage of questions. Ruthie loved Troy, so the calls and questions did not bother her at all. She knew why he tried to be so strict, she knew he knew how wrong he was. Her only wish is that he realizes that she does not hold any type of grudge against him, she understands and she loves him. There were times when she got busy with students and did not have time to call Troy and he got busy at work and failed to call her, then she began to wonder if something was wrong. Sooner or later he will call wondering why she had not called him.

One day she felt a little squeezy, she let her class go early and went by Troy's office. When Troy had a lot on his mind and a lot of work to do he closed himself up in his office. Troy had a nice secretary, she was with the company for many years. She liked Ruthie because she was down to earth and quite pleasant. She was busy when Ruthie walked up and did not notice her right away.

"Hello Irene."

"Mrs. Thompson, how are you?"

"Find thanks, is my husband in? I want to surprise him, by the way Irene, my name is still Ruthie. Talk to you when I come out."

Ruthie walked over to the door and quietly let herself in. Troy had his back to the door and so deep in his work he did not hear her come in. She put her arms around his neck and he immediately turned around.

"Honey, what are you doing here? And why aren't you working?"

"One question at a time. I wanted to come visit my husband so I dismissed my class early."

"Just like that huh?"

"Just like that."

Ruthie spent the balance of the day with Troy. She helped him with a lot of his paperwork. She knew all about the company because she spent enough time with Troy there over the years.

Just being with him, she felt a little better but did not tell him the real reason she left the campus. Ruthie had walked from her office to the class and about midway her class she had gotten so dizzy. She had to sit down. When she felt a little better she got up, again the same feeling came back so she decided to call it a day. She was glad it was her last class for the day.

"Class I think I will let you go now because I don't feel well. Your lesson will continue as before. Study the next section because you will have a test in two weeks. If you have any problems I will be here for the next ten minutes, if not, you may leave. By the way, I hope each of you have your uniforms because we will be going into the hospital in exactly three weeks and you will be assigned patients and you must know what you are doing because the nurses will be watching you all very closely. Okay, see you all tomorrow.

Ruthie was one of the better instructors in the nursing program at the college. Her class was always filled. The students learned well with her. She was very conscientious about her duties as an instructor. She never criticized, she complimented, she did not talk down to the students, she talked to them. She does not just tell them to do something, she shows them and gives them the space and time to practice until it is done properly. Learning came easy to her because she over- prepared, but everyone will not do the same.

After being away from Ruthie for such a long time, Troy looks for every opportunity to be with her. They had been back together for about three month and there was not one night Troy spent any time with the boys, nor did he allow her to go out without him. If she had, I mean really had to return to the campus for any reason, he was right there with her, regardless of what else he had planned.

The following week Ruthie came home early because she became ill again. Troy found out that she went home, he took off the balance of the day as well. Ruthie still had not told him about the dizzy spells. She tried to compose herself when she found out he was coming home. She met him at the door when she saw him drive up. Troy took her in his arms. While they were locked in each other's arms their youngest daughter came in.

"Hi Mommy, Daddy, can we talk?"

"Sure Honey, want to right now, ? We have time before I start dinner."

"I see you two all the time hugging each other. How can you keep doing that, doesn't it makes you feel funny?" Ruthie looked at Troy and mumbled. "UH, UH what's next?"

"What do you mean, honey?"

"Well, you two are married, I guess it doesn't matter.........Mommy did you and Daddy do a lot of hugging for long periods of time before you were married?"

"Yes, sometimes."

"Did it make you feel needed?"

"Yes."

"Daddy, did you like to hold Mommy in your arms real close to you?"

"Yes, I did and I did it as often as she let me."

"Did you get angry with her if she pushed you away?"

"Yes, sometimes."

"Mommy did Daddy asked you to have sex?"

"Yes, sometimes?"

"Did you?"

"No."

"Did you love him a lot?"

"Yes, I loved him very much."

"Did he get angry with you, but I still said no."

"Daddy, did you get real angry when Mommy said no?"

"Yes, as a matter of fact, I did, but because I loved her so much and after we got married I was glad she said no."

"If you love each other so much, why didn't you say yes, before you got married?"

"Honey, if I had allowed that to happen and we broke up, what would happen if the next guy came along and I did the same thing? So the next guy came along and the same thing happened. Then the next guy really wanted to marry me, he would wonder what kind of person I was, laying around with every guy I met. Somewhere down the line a really nice guy would not consider marrying me because he may see me as a tramp and lose respect for me. I wanted to be loved and respected. Loved by one guy and respected by everyone else."

"Honey, I loved Mommy very much and I would get so angry with her, but when we got married, she was so special to me because she waited. I went out with other girls before we met and I would not consider marrying any of them. I was always wondering who they laid around with before me. It is true I would get very angry with her and I even quit her one time and went out with another girl but I could not get her out of my mind. When I came to myself, I knew I had to have her at any cost. When I got her back, I still tried to get what I wanted but I knew she was the love of my life and she was going to marry me. Because she was who I wanted, I was willing to wait, but not too long. Honey you must understand, if a person truly loves you enough he will wait until you say yes to his desires and commands. Does that answer your questions?"

"I hope my boyfriend will love me as much as you love Mommy, Daddy."

"Honey, remember one thing, if your boyfriend makes unrealistic demands on you, you cannot prove he will continue to love you, if you submit yourself to him. That is why a lot of girls are lugging babies around are having abortions in record numbers. We love you very much and don't want to see you get hurt. We cannot be around, always holding your hands, so whatever you do will affect us but it will hurt you much more."

"Thanks Mom, Dad, I love you very much. What's for dinner? Can I help?"

"I suppose it's time for us to find out, and you can help and so can Daddy."

Three month after they remarried, Ruthie found out she was pregnant. When she told Troy, he was overjoyed.

"Honey, that's what is supposed to happen to newly married couples and I don't want to hear anything about age nor it may affect the baby. Another thing, none of those tests, understand?" (Holding Ruthie in his arms and sliding his hands up and down her back) Honey, with the love we share, nothing can ever be wrong with any of our children."

"But Troy, it's a normal procedure"

"No butts about it, understand?,... Do you understand?"

"Yes, Husband Troy, Sir."

"Prove it." (Her proof was a kiss)

Right away Ruthie started to gain more weight than normal. She had a hard time convincing Troy to allow her to work past two month, Into her pregnancy. He made her give up patient care in the hospital, even though she only worked two days weekly. She really only helped out because the students did the work. Troy would only agree for her to work at the college.

Ruthie was in her office on campus, one day when the air conditioner broke. The classrooms were okay but her office was steaming. She was in her office no more than five minutes when she almost passed out from the heat. Todd had seen her enter the building and he followed her. He wanted to talk to her, he never had the chance, only that one time when she sneaked away from Troy to apologize for not going through with their wedding plans. When Todd walked into her office, Ruthie was leaning against the wall, holding her head. Todd put his arms around her and walked her out to the water cooler, took his handkerchief, wet it and applied some cool water to her forehead and face.

"You sit down right here and tell me what you need out of your office and I will get it for you. I want to get you to a cooler place.

"Thanks Todd, I will be alright."

"Look, young lady, did you hear what I say? I am not leaving you here alone. I don't want anything to happen to those babies you are carrying because they were supposed to be mine.

"Babies? … where did you get that idea?"

"Baby, I bet you any amount of money that you are carrying more than one."

"Todd, you are joking."

"Uh, uh, I have been watching you real closely lately."

"Todd, can I ask you something and I need an honest answer."

"Shoot?"

"If someone loves you and tells you not to do something and you do it anyway, because they feel it should be done and you found out, would you be real angry with them, I mean real angry?"

"Yes and I would probably break their neck."

"Oh, you men."

"What's wrong, Troy doesn't want you to see if the babies may have any sort of mental problems because of your age? If you were my wife and as much as I love you, I wouldn't let you be tested either."

"I can't even get support from a Doctor and he should know how I feel."

"Look, tell me what you need so I can get you to a cooler place."

Ruthie was somewhat uneasy about the thought of having twins at her age. She just knew Todd was wrong, but she had gotten much larger earlier than she did with her other children. She thought; "twins?" ,…" I wonder how Troy will feel about that?" I better not mention it especially if I told him that was what Todd said, he would really get angry." Ruthie looked over at Todd, she thought how gentle and willing to please he was the times they went out together. He never placed any demands on her. She knew he wanted to but she denied his advances every time. She thought that was the reason he wanted to rush into marriage. She had no idea Troy had told him he was taking her back at any cost. Todd came over with the things she asked him to get for her from her office. "Here you are, young lady, now let's get out of here."

"Thanks Todd, I'm okay now."

"Let me be the judge of that, I am the doctor, remember?"

When Ruthie was in her third month of pregnancy, Troy began to really notice how big she was getting.

"Baby, after this month you will be staying home. Do you want to explain to the Dean or do you want me too?"

"Honey, I want to finish the next semester, I am not doing anything."

"Baby, I said......"

"I know what you said, but you are not listening to me....... Honey, I know what is best for me.. "

"And I don't?"

"I didn't mean that."

"Then tell me what you meant?"

"I don't want to stay home all day every day alone."

"What makes you think you will be home everyday alone?"

"Well, you have to work, anyway we don't want the children to spend the rest of their lives repaying student loans and my salary is taking care of the tuition for two of them right now, "

"I know Baby, but I have that under control, believe me. Remember those investments we made for each child when they were born? Well I checked on them the other day. I believe it is time to cash them in. It's enough there for T. J. Amber and Lois to complete their education. We will be okay by the time Larry, Gravina and Thesa get in college and (Troy puts his hands on Ruthie's belly) these guys." Ruthie put her hands on Troy's, "What do you mean, these guys?"

"I was talking to the doctor the other day about your weight gain and he has scheduled you for an ultrasound. He thinks you may be carrying more than one baby."

"Honey, are you kidding me?" "Twins?, Triplets" or, ?"

"Stop right there Baby, don't get carried away. Let's start with twins and hope that is all the ultrasound shows." However, I will be overjoyed with whatever number is in this belly. I am going to plan on taking a leave from my job and stay home with you when the baby or babies are born, if you want me to or not.

"Honey, now back to my job, I would like to continue working."

"Baby you don't have to work. Look, my salary is almost clear, we don't have any bills other than utilities, food and other little things we like to purchase from time to time, lawn care, etc etc."

"Honey, I know that but my students are depending on me to be there for them until they graduate."

"Baby, I said, next month and that will be that, any more questions on the subject? By the way, I made an appointment for you to see the doctor tomorrow at ten, is that alright?"

"I don't believe you."

"Believe it Baby, believe it. Come on, don't be angry with me. I am just so anxious to hear the heart beats of our babies. Believe me Baby, I love you so much. I don't believe you realize how much I love you and how happy you have made me since the first day I met you.

Ruthie gave birth to two healthy little boys. Troy claimed total resembleness but Ruthie had two claims, each of them had her birthmark on their shoulder, in the same place as her's. Also T. J. also had her birthmark in the same place. None of the other children had any kind of birthmark. T. J. and the twin did bear almost total resemblance to Troy. All the girls looked much like Ruthie and all their children had a little bit of each parent likeness.

They never held anything against their father for the time he was away from them, in fact, they never discuss it but that one time they did as a family when he ask them to forgive him, because he must have been overwhelm as a result of his parents placing demands on him and he must have felt guilty because he was neglecting his family. He always felt that parents were very important and when their needs rose, he thought it most important to take care of their needs.

At that time he told his children to never neglect your family for me and your mother. We gave birth to you because of our love for you, not because you are supposed to take care of us when we get old. He told them that right now your Mom and I are supposed to be making plans for our old age and not expecting you to care for us. We as parents were and are required to care for you and not expect the same from you. Always remember what I just said and never feel guilty because you forgot to send a greeting card, call on special days or bring or send a gift, that is not the reason you were born. I also want you to know if any of you need us for anything do not hesitate to ask. All of you are here because we love you and want you to be a part of our family.

CHAPTER 22

●●···························●

"I was all set to spend the weekend with some friends and here comes mother. "Troy I am sorry but you have to stay with Carrie and Susan, your Dad and I have to go to a banquet tonight." I was so angry and embarrassed, then you walked into my life and rescued me. From that moment on I felt out of place with other girls."

You know so many things are happening on the college campuses today. I don't want anything to go wrong. Do you understand Baby? Come here, please, I love you so much."

"Oh Troy, don't ever stop loving me."

"You don't have to worry about that, I am hooked on you."

The following day Troy took Ruthie to the doctor. When the doctor told them he heard two heartbeats, Troy was so happy, he had a smile which ran across his face from ear to ear, and from chin to his forehead all in one facial expression. Right there in the office he took Ruthie in his arms. "Baby, baby I love you, did you hear what I said? After a short while he calmed down. He took Ruthie home and took off from work the rest of the day. Troy made lunch and afterward made Ruthie lay down for a nap.

Later that evening Gloria called to tell Ruthie her Dad was ill and needed surgery, which he was refusing. She explained to Troy what Gloria had said.

"Troy, Honey would you mind if I go spend a few days with my dad and try talking to him? It is important to me?"

"Yes, I would mind, if you spend a few days. I will drive you there as soon as you get dressed and we will be back home tonight."

"Okay Honey, Let's wait until the children get home from school, maybe they would like to come along."

Ruthie's Dad was in pain but he felt a pill would serve the purpose and that would be all he needed. Ruthie tried to talk to him and explain why surgery is the best thing for him. He still refused.

"Alright Dad, if you just cannot understand how important this surgery is I will talk to the doctor and find out if there is any other alternative other than surgery and see what he suggest"

Mr. Warren knowing what a good nurse and college Instructor Ruthie was, he felt, she could do something no one else could. He knew she loved him as a father regardless of what had happened in the past because she had demonstrated her love and concern for him more than once. There was a time when he and Gloria were in a financial bind because of a problem with Gloria's daughter and they almost lost their home. It so happened that Ruthie came by for a visit. He was on the phone trying to talk the bank out of foreclosure on his home and Ruthie overheard him. "Dad, what is wrong? I could not but overhear what you were talking about on the telephone. I would be more than happy to help in any way I can."

"Child, I don't think there is anything you can do about this problem, because I need ten thousand dollars like yesterday." Ruthie still had most of the money in the bank from the Carters, she had not had to use much of it because of her other bank account and her job and the scholarships she received. She did very little running around, purchasing things she did not need and wasting money. She looked at her Dad and smiled, "Dad do you mind if I check with the bank tomorrow? I do believe I can help. Do you think they can wait that long? Better still, let me give them a call." Ruthie called the bank and asked to come in the next day to discuss her father's account. They agreed but she must make sure her father comes in with her. She had Troy take her home and the next day she went to the bank and withdrew ten thousand dollars and deposited it in her checking account. She took the bus over to her father's house and they along with Gloria went to the bank. Mr. Warren was surprised to know that Ruthie had that much money. He really had not expected what was to come. He offered to put her name on the deed to his house but she refused. "No Dad, I did not do what I just did for that reason, I only wanted to help. You can pay me back half of it if you become a millionaire, in the very near future and besides, the GOD I serve, teaches that you do not give to receive, you do what you can to help someone also, because you love them. That money was given to me to further my education, if I needed it and I am using what I need." Mr. Warren knew that Ruthie was the only one of the children who bothered to send him and Gloria cards and gifts on special days. Sometimes on his birthday, Father day and Christmas he might get a card from some of the other children, but not on a regular basis, as for Gloria, she never received anything from the children other than Ruthie. Mr. Warren did not want to use her money but at that time he had no other choice unless they became homeless. He had been ill and Gloria would not work in a 'pie factory' She felt she worked enough when she was married the first time and had the children. She had to hold down a job, take care of the children and household responsibilities. When she got out of such a bad marriage, she vowed to never work outside the home again. When she met Chris Warren, she told him, up front, that she will never go to work regardless of "what?" He accepted the relationship on those bases. She felt that if they went down, they would go down together because she was not going to try to lift anyone up.

That night after Ruthie paid all the bills, Chris asked her about getting a job so they could repay Ruthie, they had the fight of their life and did not speak to each other for days. After that when Ruthie went over they started to act kind of funny, so that was the reason Troy did not think very much of them.

"Honey I know that is your father, but I think they have used you, so now they cannot face you. It seems like every time we go over, they think you want something. Why don't you stop going over for a while and let them make an effort to contact you. I bet you, if they need you for any- thing, you will hear from them."

"Oh, Troy I don't think they feel that way, I am not worried about that money because I told my father if he becomes a millionaire he can repay me half of the money. I am sure he doesn't feel that way."

As time passed, Ruthie began to notice many little insignificant things and some very significant things in her relationship with them. Soon she did not need words to tell her to stay away.

When Ruthie was to get married she wanted her family there, and they did come, but afterward she heard very little from them. She never stopped sending gifts and greetings on special days and nothing was returned to her. The few times she saw them when they had money problems. Ruthie met her sister Lana one day while she was shopping with a friend and she came running over to her. "Ruthie, is that you? Boy do you look good. I am sorry I haven gotten in touch with you to thank you for the gifts you sent, but I have been having so many problems."

"Well, how are the children? I know they are quite grown up now"

"Yes, they are fine and they keep me broke because they are at that age where they need first one thing and then another. I am trying to find some things for them right now because they are in some activities at school and need some special things. How is Troy? You two aren't going to have any children? Are you still in your apartment?"

"Troy is fine and we have a little boy and I am two month pregnant now. Why don't you come over and see our house, we have been in it for a few years now and you can get to meet my son."

"Sure, why not? I got all day, almost."

Lana was elated when she saw Ruthie's home. It had all of the things she dreamed of and saw in magazines. "Ruthie, this is your home? I bet this cost a fortune, I would not want to make your mortgage payments."

"We do not have mortgage payments. We paid cash for our home before we moved in." Ruthie explained to Lana about the decision they made about no mortgage, no children, no bills and only taxes and utility and normal things needed and all other money saved for our children's education.

"Troy must be rich."

"Not really Lana, it was a joint effort between the two of us."

"That guy must be crazy about you."

"We are very much in love with each other."

Lana determines that Ruthie had so much, she thought it would be a good time to get a few dollars to help get the things she needed for her children.

"Ruthie would you, if you can, loan me a few dollars? I got to find that dress for my daughter, I saw it in one store and I don't have enough money with me."

"Sure Lana, what do you need?"

"What do I need? Don't ask that question. I need about a thousand dollars, but I will settle for fifty."

"Are you sure that would be enough?"

"Enough or not, it's what I can deal with."

"I can give you the money but why don't you do this. I will go shopping with you otherwise I will have to go to the bank. Troy will be home shortly. I can see what money he has. I don't usually have money around the house, maybe five dollars or so. We can go shopping after lunch."

"Find with me."

Troy had about a hundred dollars on him, so Ruthie took that. Ruthie ended up spending about eight hundred dollars that day plus she gave Lana five hundred dollars she truly needed.

Over the years Ruthie always runs into one of her siblings and they always have some sort of "GREAT" financial need and she being Ruthie, would reach out to them. Ruthie had a great spirit about her. When she was going through her many trials and tribulations in her life very few people were there for her, but there was that someone always by her side, directing her to a path of the direction she should go and when she listened and obeyed her path of direction alway ended up in the right places. It seemed like her reaction timing was always at the right time, even when others tried to harm her and she did not want to cause harm to them her reaction was just at the right moment and she cause no real harm to the other person. The time she had to free herself from Bob Brene, he held her so tight until she could not free herself without trying one last push, she had the energy to hit him in the right place, which took him to his knees but he was not hurt seriously. Her timing with Mr Crossley kept and reminded him who he should be. Her life with the Carters help prepared her for the challenging life she had to be faced with. Her love for Troy and his love for her was lasting because she stood her grounds with him. Her own father turned his back on her and she still shows her love for him and her siblings. What more of a challenge can a little girl have, if there was not a Supreme Being at her side. Ruthie knew who she was and she stood her grounds. She did not allow negatives to change her ways. It didn't matter to her if 'everybody was doing it' she knew she would not allow herself to do what everybody else was doing, because that "BEING" who stood beside her said "that is wrong" If we only take a moment to listen to the message being taught we would have less problems. Rest assure these messages, most times are not verbal, they are spiritual. Those of us who have read the Scriptures know that there is a Supreme Being that is the head of our lives and we cannot see Him, yet He speaks to us. Also there are many who do not believe and they go along doing whatever they feel like and that causes many problems to all concern Ruthie faced many problems but she was able to deal with them because she believed. We must understand that issues and problems never end. We merely have to know who we are and all things will work out in time.

CHAPTER 23

•·····················•

Ruthie contacted the doctor for her father, just to console him because she knew there was no medication which would relieve him of pain, only surgery would help. Troy got angry with Ruthie because it seemed her family was always calling her with their problems and not once since they were married did they elect to come visit, just to visit. It was always to complain about one or the other borrowing something which they never pay back. When each child was born, Ruthie always sent out announcements, not once did they call to congratulate them. He did not want to hurt his wife but, if that is what he had to do to make her face reality, so be it.

When they left her father's house that day even he knew that surgery was the only answer to her father's problem.

"Honey, why are you leading your father on? You know what any doctor would say, at this point."

"Yes, I understand what you mean. I just want to talk to the doctor anyway before I say anything definite to him."

"Honey, for the life of me, I cannot understand why you allow your family to use you as they do, personally, I am getting tired of it. I am trying my best not to tell them what's on my mind. Either you tell them you are no longer going to be around for them each time they have a need are I will and I don't think they will like the way I say it. You know I don't mind the way you spend money or share anything we have, it's just that I want you to receive some consideration, by the same people that you are issuing these favors to. We love our children and they love each other. We can see that. I am sorry to say Honey, but with your Father, Sisters, and Brothers, I cannot say the same. I think you know how I feel and have felt for a long time. You are going to stop with the favors, understand?"

"Yes, I understand. I have been saying that to myself for a long time, because of illness, I thought I should go. I wasn't trying to buy their friendship nor their love, I only wanted to prove to them that regardless of how they felt about me, I could still love them and I do Honey, I do."

"I know that Baby, that is one of the reasons I love you so much. When my parents were treating you like dirt, the only thing you did was prove how much you loved them. Mother often talks about you when we are alone. She constantly tells me how much she loves you and how lucky I am. I tell her over and over again that I knew how lucky I was to have met you and I never pick a loser in anything I do are anyone I select. She tells me I am being facetious, what do you think Honey?"

"I think she is right."

"I don't believe this, my own wife." Troy put his arms around Ruthie and they drove home.

Ruthie was pregnant with her ninth child. Troy was happy because he was getting closer to the ten he wanted. Ruthie believing she was too old was a little upset, but Troy soon stopped those thoughts. Ruthie could see how proud he was because he took to the telephone calling his friends and bragging about his wife. They had been so very fortunate, their children were all handsome, beautiful, intelligent and healthy. They received so much love and understanding from their parents, they had no need to seek after any artificial substance to fulfill their lives.

Troy decided to take Ruthie out to a dinner party which was given by one of the guys from his office. Troy pulled up in front of the house to let Ruthie out before he parked the car, which was what everybody else was doing because they had to park their cars in the back of the house. He got out of the car and started to walk around the other side to open the door for Ruthie. He had not seen the car coming at a high rate of speed, just about time he got to the rear of the car the oncoming car slammed, broadside into his car, Ruthie was pinned down in the car, she could not move. Troy was like a mad man trying to get his wife out of the car. Within minutes help was available. Somehow or another Todd managed to get himself invited to many of the affairs Ruthie was to attend, he had a way of finding out this information. He was still very much in love with Ruthie. Even though he got married and had a few children, he still would try to see Ruthie anytime he could. So when someone came into the house and told them Troy's wife was pinned in the car, he ran out like a mad man, not caring who he pushed out of the way. The only thing that slowed him down was when he saw Troy and realized that he was her husband. Troy was talking to Ruthie while the others were trying to free her. All the workmen had on fireproof outfits but Todd. He was working harder than the others. He reached Ruthie and pulled her out. He and Troy carried her far away from the car. He looked at Troy and said, "I think we better take her to the hospital right away, she's expecting isn't she?" Troy looked at him with a puzzle in his eye, as if to say, how did you know?" Todd, being a medical doctor, knew what to do. He said I will get my car and we can take her, there's no need to wait for an ambulance, we can make better time." Troy knew if that car had exploded he would want to die if it killed Ruthie. So when Todd walked over he spoke.

"Is she alright?" Troy looked at Todd.

"No, she is not alright." He called Ruthie, again.

"Honey, do you hear?" A faint voice answered.

"Honey my belly hurts real bad." Will they get me out soon?"

Todd leaned over trying to see if he could see Ruthie.

"Ruthie, is there anything pressing on your stomach?"

"Yes, that is why I can't move" Troy looked over at Todd and spoke.

"Should she be talking so much?"

"Yes, to keep her mind off herself." Within fifteen minutes Ruthie was freed and no sooner than they got her out the car exploded. Ruthie was rushed to the hospital. Troy on one side and Todd on the other. Her belly hurt a bit because of the bruises but the baby was fine, they could hear the heartbeat. Ruthie remained in the hospital a few days just to make sure everything was alright. The children were in and out, Troy was there when he was not working. He would fall asleep with Ruthie in his arms. He would go home, take a shower and to work or at the hospital.

Carrie and his mother were at the house most of the time to make sure the children had what they needed.

After a few weeks everything had gotten back to normal in the household. Ruthie was back to her old self it seemed. She begins to get bored sitting around. One day she decided to drive up to the college to visit the faculty members she knew and worked with from time to time.

When she went into the Nursing Department she was delighted that some of the Freshman

Whom she had known addressed her as Professor Thompson. When she went into the main office she saw a large picture of her hanging there among the other professors. Ruthie vaguely remembered that the college did call her to notify that they were honoring her but Troy would not let her go because she was very much pregnant, expecting to deliver any time. She believed he responded to the college for her. When Ruthie walked into the office most of the people addressed her as if nothing had changed. She stayed around for about an hour chatting. Most of the staff had kept tabs on her so she could not fill them in on much of anything about her life because they already knew most of it. When she was in that accident she got cards from so many people she did not know. She sent a thank you card but was waiting to say thank you in person to them to all she could.

After Ruthie left the campus she met Troy for lunch. He was not expecting her so she found him quite busy with some business associates. She was surprised to find a new receptionist there.

Troy's receptionist of many years had become ill and could no longer work. It happened during the time Ruthie was in the accident. When

Ruthie walked in to the reception desk and attempted to go right in Troy's office, she spoke up. "I am sorry Miss, but Mr. Thompson is with someone and you cannot go in there, just have a seat, he should be out soon." Not saying a word to let her know who she was, Ruthie picked up a magazine and sat down in the lobby outside Troy's office. Renee had only been there a few days and was learning. Before too long Troy came out of his office along with his business associates. They wanted him to go to lunch with them.

"I would love to but I may have to run home. I have been trying to get my wife but she has not answered my call. At that time Renee the receptionist handed him his messages. Mr Thompson your wife called, here are the other messages, also there is a young lady waiting to see you. Troy turned, seeing that it was his wife, he walked over, put his arms around her and kissed her.

"Honey, why did you come into the office?" (Whispering in his ear)" Your receptionist said I could not and for me to wait.

"Well, we will straighten that out right now." Troy took one step and realized. "When did anybody ever stop you from coming into my office?" Ruthie smiled and he gave her another kiss. "Baby, what were you doing over at the college? Not thinking about what I am thinking, if so the answer is no."

"Honey?"

"No"

"Anyway, I only went by to thank them for the many cards and flowers, that's all."

"It better be, Honey, let's go home for a while, I want to talk to you."

"I have seen that look in your eyes and I have heard that phrase before about a thousand times."

"Only a thousand times, that's all?" Troy took Ruthie home and he did not get back to the office until about an hour before it was too close.

Six months after Ruthie gave birth to her ninth child, she became pregnant with a second set of twins. She was excited in a way and Troy was overjoyed. He was so proud and over protective of her. Whenever he could he would have her come to work with him. Most times pretending he needed her help. He merely wanted to make sure she was not doing too much, especially when there were three small children at home. They never forced the other children to watch over the younger one, they merely did it on their own. Troy hired a nursemaid to help out at their home, but most times she had very little to do because when the other children came home, they took charge. They had a game room with everything imaginable for the young ones. None of the children were required to change diapers, now that was an adult job. T. J. and his wife were always over as well as Amber and Lois and their husbands. All three of them had gotten married.

T. J. and his wife were living in the apartment Ruthie lived in at the Thompson's, Amber and her husband lived with her Grandmother, and Lois and her Husband lived with Carrie. T'. J. was in medical school as well as Amber, Lois wanted to become a Nurse. They all were doing well. T. J. and Amber had a few more years before they completed their degrees. With their scholarships and jobs they rarely seek help from their parents. All three of them seem to be following the path of their parents. No home and no children until they complete some of the goals they establish for themselves. Ruthie often prepared meals for them.

Ruthie thought Troy was joking when she asked him why he was having a five bedroom house built. He said, for our children". Well he wanted ten children and she is about to give him his eleven. She felt that, is going to be 'IT' whether he knew it or not. Troy watches every little thing she does and constantly questions her on how she is feeling. He tends to be overly concerned about her feelings and things she is doing on a daily basis. He did not want her to drive her car or go out alone. He is constantly popping in from work to check on her. Ruthie has been worrying about him more. She is constantly trying to convey to him that she is alright and stop worrying, she will be alright.

Ruthie never had any problems with pregnancies. She has always eaten the right things, exercised and slept well. Nor did she allow 'things' to bother her. She loved herself as well as others. If she found that others did not care about her for any reason, she merely loved them and leave them alone. She learned in life that you cannot force anyone to love you and why should you worry if they don't, because that is a choice they made. As much as she loved Troy when he made decisions to walk away she never tried to fight for his affection. She let him know her feelings and moved on. When he came to his senses he asked for her to forgive him because he loved her.

Troy was fully aware of his wife's beauty and abilities, which had changed very little over the years, that was why he kept her close and pregnant, as often as he possibly could. Even with that he was insanely jealous, but able to control his insanity from the surface. Each time when Ruthie talked about returning to work, Troy got upset. He knew Todd was still in love with Ruthie. He could tell the way he watched her. He also told him so when she was in that accident. Todd still lectured at the college and was still on staff at the hospital. Troy did not want Ruthie around the college nor did he want her working at the hospital.

CHAPTER 24

———◆ ·············· ◆———

Ruthie's Dad had managed to hold off from having the operation, but things were getting worse and he had been finding it harder to deal with the pain. The exercise and medication no longer worked. Mr. Warren still would not agree to the surgery. Ruthie tried to comfort him as much as she could, along with the doctor, they reached a point where only surgery would be his only relief. Mr Warren had his wife Gloria call Ruthie to see what could be done this time. Ruthie was in the shower when she called. Thesa answered the telephone.

"Hello, Granda Glo."

"Hello Thesa, let me talk to your mother, please?"

"She's in the shower, can I take a message?"

"Tell her to call me as soon as she gets out of the shower."

"Okay, I will. Bye now."

Troy drove Ruthie to her father's house. When they got there he was asleep on the couch. Gloria was preparing dinner. Troy rang the doorbell.

"Hi, I am glad you could come. Maybe this time you can make him do something which should have done a year ago."

"How have you been Gloria? You know this is something he has to make up his mind to have done and the only thing we can do is to encourage him."

"Yeh, I know, that man is so stubborn, so set in his ways, you are the only one he listens to. I can't understand because you are the child who he......... done the least for." Gloria caught herself. What she wanted to say was, you are the only child by his wife who he didn't believe he fathered. She tried to clear herself. "What I mean is that you are the youngest and did not live with them that much. I guess it's because you are the only one who successfully made something of yourself and your life. A rich husband, nine wonderful bright children and a good education for yourself. We haven't forgotten about the money we owe you."

"Money? Gloria, you folks do not owe me anything. I told Dad that when I gave it to him. You folks did not ask to borrow, I offered it to you. Do you understand Lady?" All the while Troy was watching the guilty look on Gloria's face. He wondered what she was thinking. He only wanted Ruthie's dad to wake up so they could get away from there.

They were there about a half an hour before he woke up. He got up greeting Ruthie and Troy and went to the bathroom. When he returned he was holding his back. Troy led him to his bed, while Ruthie lectured Gloria how to rub his back.

Dad, now look, you have suffered long enough and nothing else is going to ease your pain because you need the operation in order to remove what it is that is pressing on that nerve..."

"Okay, okay, thanks Ruthie, I know what you are trying to say, but....."

"No buts about it, dad, I am serious."

"Ruthie, would you rub my back? You are a nurse and you know the right areas to massage."

"Oh dad, Gloria is doing a good job of it, I have been watching her."

"Let me be the judge of that, come on, give it a try."

"Okay." Ruthie began to rub her dad's back and she noticed his birthmark.

"You know dad, I see your birthmark and you know something, I have the same birthmark in the very same spot and so does my son T. J. and my two twin boys."

Mr Warren quickly turned over on his back and looked up at Ruthie, staring up at her as if all the pain he had left.

"O my God, what have I done? What have I done?"

"Dad, what's wrong?"

"You are my child, you really are my child. Oh my God, please forgive me."

"Dad, what are you talking about?" Mr Warren realized he had let the 'cat-out-of-the-bag, so to speak. He went on to explain that he had not believed Ruthie was his child, that was why he made her mother give her up. He thought she was messing around. Ruthie's mother was a very attractive woman and wherever she went men as well as women would turn their heads for a second or third glance. He went on to tell them about a neighbor who would always find his way over to their house, not believing his wife when she told him that she never let him in. Elene, Ruthie's mother, was a high fashion model before she married Chris Warren. She alway kept herself looking good. She gave up her career for Chris Warren because she fell in love with him. When they married He demand that she give up her career and she did because she loved him.

Mr. Warren admitted that he was blindly jealous and would accuse her constantly of messing around. In the early years of their marriage he kept her pregnant. After the fifth child it appeared that she could not have anymore. They tried but she had a miscarriage before Ruthie was born.

After the miscarriage, Chris told every body he could not father anymore children. Elene was not healthy enough either. He was quite upset about the loss of their child. He blamed himself, so he withdrew himself from his wife and they only slept together maybe once a week. Things got kind of rough and Elene had to get a job. She had a degree in elementary education so she got a job teaching. Chris was unhappy about this but they had no choice. His job was iffy and they had five children to support.

After about three years Chris' job picked up again and they were on easy street. Elene got pregnant with Ruthie. He just knew the baby was not his. He did not take the time to find out if the child was his. Elene gave Ruthie to her sister when she was an infant, just to keep the peace in their home. Ruthie's aunt kept her for two years. Her husband was injured at work and she had to provide total care for him, so she gave Ruthie back to her mother. From there Ruthie's grandmother kept her for about two years until she became disabled and unable to care for her because her eyesight was failing. Elene tried to keep Ruthie in the family with hopes that one day Chris would realize that Ruthie was his child and she never went out with any men. She loved Chris very much and never thought of going out with any other men. When she was at home Chris would accuse her of any and every little thing. He did not seem to want her in his sight. She constantly wishes for that day when Chris would know that Ruthie was his child. Elene knew she was faithful to her husband and she loved him very much. Her love for Chris and the breakup of their marriage as well as the guilt of giving up her child was what caused her death.

Before they left the house Mr Warren had agreed to have the surgery. As soon as all the arrangements were made Ruthie had agreed to be there. Troy was thinking. "Yes, she will be there, if I bring her." Troy was never that fond of Chris Warren, because of what they put a little innocent child through, now he disliked him even more because it seems like he was responsible for his wife's death also. He was only nice to him because of Ruthie. Troy tried to think of how he would handle that situation if it had occurred with him and Ruthie. He felt that he would have loved the child as his own because it was not the fault of the child whose sperm caused it to develop. He looked over at Ruthie and smiled.

"Honey, are you happy, now that you know why you were placed in Homes away from home?"

No, I am not sure how I feel right now because my own father did not try to know me. It's hard to believe that he never really tried to see me to know me, and believed my mother when she told him I was his child. She must have loved him more than anybody, to give up her child to prove herself to him. Even then they still broke up. How could she have done such a thing?"

"Gosh, neither one of my parents really loved me, nor did they really care what happened to me." As the tears rolled down Ruthie's cheek. "Honey I am so glad you love me, please don't ever stop because if you do, I don't know what I will do" Troy pulled the car over to the side of the road and cuddled her in his arms. "Baby, I could never stop loving you and don't you forget it and don't you forget, you have a lot of others who love you as well. Another thing is, don'tforget you have a couple others that's going to love you in a few months, laying around in your belly just waiting to meet you."

Ruthie had made up her mind that she was going to do everything she could to see her father through the surgery and make sure he was alright and then she would never call him again. If he wants to talk to her he will call.

She made all the arrangements, he was operated on three day later. She was there when he went into surgery and when he came out. Troy made a reservation at a nearby hotel for her to stay and a driver to take her back and forth to the hospital for two days. He sensed that it was something she wanted to do and he gave her no argument, but two days was his limit she would be away. Ruthie was pleased with that. Troy called her a few times each day and she called him. After the second day Troy came to pick her up and he did not bother to visit Chris Warren, nor did he ask her about him. When Troy came she was ready. She was very quiet. She put her arms around his neck. "Thank Honey, I am ready to go home to my family."

CHAPTER 25

●••••••••••••••••••••••••••••••••••●

Marlo had contacted Ruthie shortly after T. J borned, she wanted to know if Ruthie would be her Matron of Honor in her wedding. Ruthie was overjoyed, but Troy didn't want her out -and-about so early after their first child. Ruthie had given him all the reason why she should but he was still a bit reluctant. Marlo had come a long way. Her life was a tremendous tragedy. Both her parents died as a result of drug overdoses. She was an only child and very much out of control. None of her relatives wanted to provide care for her. She herself was into drugs at an early age. She was placed into foster care at about age twelve. When her parents were arrested. Marlo's grandparents lived across the country and were not aware of what was happening to their daughter, nor her grandchild. In fact Marlo was unaware of where they lived. Because of their lifestyle they kept their distance. Marlo's mother got involved with her father while she was away at college and once she graduated she decided to relocate where her father lived and they got married. Marlo's grandfather was unable to do a lot of traveling so they rarely saw their daughter. They might have seen Marlo once or twice since the day she was born. Marlo's mother, Kimberly, was an educator. She taught school for about three years after Marlo was born. Her father, Joseph could not find the job he felt he deserved, so just any job was not pleasing to him. He would get hired on a job and right away he tried to be the Boss telling them how to run their business. He became so frustrated with the way his life was leading, he started handing out with the wrong crowd and started selling drugs and later started using them as well.

Then he coerced Kimberly to get high with him. She soon lost her job as a teacher. Marlo was bounced around to so many places and someone showed some concern by contacting the child protective agency. Her parents were arrested for child neglecting and drugs were found in their home. About a year later they both were found dead in their apartment. Marlo never found out how they died. She believed her grandparents may have claimed their bodies and had them buried where they lived. She knew very little about her father's family. What she knew about her mother's parents was that they lived on a big farm and had a big house. She believed they owned it. No one in the family has ever contacted her about anything during her childhood. She, herself, has never tried to find out anything about her family, nor did she understood where to start, if it had crossed her mind

One day out of the blue, she got a certified letter from a Lawyer, she could not imagine why until she opened it. It was concerning a "Will" left by her grandmother, and she had to be there by a certain date for the reading of it. They gave the name and address of the place in Atlanta Georgia. She has never traveled that far and where was she going to get the money from for her and Timmy? The only person she could think of was Ruthie. She knew Ruthie was the only one she could depend on, for a favor. Then she had done so much for them already, she hated to ask. "She thought, If property is involved, then she will sell it and make sure Ruthie gets paid back" Marlo called Ruthie and explained and Ruthie provided her with what she thought she needed.

Marlo's mother had one brother and the property was split in half, she knew she was cheated out of all she should have received but she just let it slide. She was given $75. 000. She said okay and thank you. She caught the next flight back home. She could see that the house itself was worth more than $75. 000. She thought, just maybe he helped took care of her grandparents while they were aging and he deserves what he will receive. She knew she could do a lot with the money. She didn't want to hang around questioning every detail and every dollar that the property and house was worth. Before she took her flight she called Ruthie and told her about the money and how much as well as her decision not to question her Uncle. Ruthie thought it was a wise decision she made and told her she might have done the same thing. Ruthie urged her to keep her finances to herself and if she decided to purchase a home, just make sure, if you ever get married and the man divorce you His name is not on the house and he cannot claim any part of it. Also, it would be a good idea to put a set amount of the money in Timmy's name, so only you or he can take it out. Ruthie told her that it is wise to keep your important paper in a safe place (a bank vault).

Marlo found a very good job after she finished her training. She had wanted to buy a house for herself and Timmy, so with the money she could. She was happy with the way her life was going and all the things she had learned. She had always felt bad about the way she treated Ruthie. She found out even with what she had done to Ruthie, Ruthie was her very best friend. Marlo met and was in school with a guy named Grant Cobbs. They were in the same class and pursuing the same type of career. They did a lot of studying together. They did many of the assigned projects together. They would call each other many evenings concerning the work they had to do for the next day. They became very dependent upon each other. Sometimes their

Home work led them into a date night. With Timmy hanging along. Timmy liked being with Grant and he liked having him. Grant worked full time and so did Marlo.

Tom Brene and his wife broke up and when he found out Marlo had bought a house he started going around trying to talk to Marlo but Marlo would have nothing to do with him. He tried to involve Timmy in the relationship but Marlo would not bend. He tried to make Marlo believe he wanted a relationship with his son but Marlo did not allow that to change her mind. Both his parents were seriously ill and they were about to lose their home. Tom would not get a job and keep up with the taxes and other bills, even when he and his wife and child live there. His daughter was mentally challenged and needed someone to provide constant care for her. His wife worked and when she did, Tom and his parents would provide the necessary care for her. When Tom told her he and his wife broke up, Marlo surmised that she got tired of taking care of him and that is why she left. Now that his parents could no longer care for the child. He can no longer pretend he was the caregiver. Marlo Allowed Tom in her house one time, when he saw how organized it was, he tried his best to talk himself into a relationship with her. Timmy had to show him his room. He had every imaginable thing a child could have. He told him "Daddy, my aunt Ruthie took me to the store and told me to pick out everything I wanted." Tom couldn't believe his eyes. He turned to Marlo, "Oh, you and Ruthie are friends now, after all the things you have done to her?" Marlo held her head up high and spoke. "Yes, when you stole my rent money and we were put out in the street, She got us a place to stay and paid our rent for six months, while I found another job and a sitter for Timmy. She was the only one who reached out and helped me." "Yeh, I heard she married a rich guy and they have quite a few children."

"No I think you got it wrong, they worked together, because she was a professor at the college and while she worked when we all lived together she was saving her money for college. When she married she had quite a bit of money herself. They worked together and saved after they got married. Troy also had a decent job and he was saving also. She made him wait almost two years before they got married."

"Yeh, what were they doing? Shacking?"

"No, Not Ruthie, she was not that kind of person."

Grant and Marlo dated for about six month, then he asked her to marry him. She was overjoyed because she truly liked him. He was kind and giving and most of all he liked Timmy and they got along well.

When Tom found out Marlo was getting married he was angry but there was nothing he could do about it. He was being sued by his wife for child support and his wife for alimony. His parents had to go into a nursing home and he ended up in a shelter for the homeless. When Marlo saw him she looked the other way and he would hang around the place he knew she would be, which was near her job. She felt bad for him because he gave the impression that the world should cater to him and all he had to do was sit and wait, because sooner or later everything would fall into his hands. Tom failed to realize that we all must earn our way and deal with the ups and downs of life and then we will reap the harvest. In other words, we plant the seeds, nourish their growth and then the harvest time will come. We must know what we bargain for and then we will have a good idea of what we will receive.

Marlo had a beautiful wedding and Ruthie was there for her. Grant seems to be just the type of guy Marlo needed. He seemed very much in love with Marlo. He didn't have a lot of friends or relatives, even though he was born and raised in the city. They went on a short honeymoon just for three days and Timmy stayed with Ruthie. Ruthie told him he was the big brother to T. J. He loved it and was always there watching over him. If T. J. grunt, he calls Ruthie.

Over the years Marlo and Grant were married, they had two children and there was never any kind of animosity between them. Grant loved all of them the same. Tom tried to intervene but Timmy alway stuck close to Grant. He chose to address him as daddy and identify him as his father.

CHAPTER 26

$\bullet\!\!-\!\cdots\cdots\cdots\cdots\cdots\cdots\cdots\cdots\!-\!\bullet$

As time passed Ruthie continued to gain more weight. She went out less and less and Troy stayed home more and more. There were many days Troy went to work and stayed long enough to see that everything and everybody was working normally then right back home he went. Sometimes Ruthie would take a walk around the yard, which was about one acres of ground and that would be her morning exercise. She managed to do that up to her eighth month. After that she walked much less. When she first went into labor it was when she was on one of her walks and Troy was with her. He was with her as always and he delivered all of his babies. He was most happy to see two little girls added to his family.

"Honey, look, both of the girls have that birthmark, but in different places. Troy, do you realize that I would have had a mother and a father if they would have taken the time to check me out, because the birthmarks are so obvious."

"Baby, then I may not have met you."

"Honey, that's not possible, regardless of what our lives would have been, we would have met somewhere, some place, somehow.

CHAPTER 27

R uthie was surprised when she picked up the telephone and heard a familiar voice, her sister Lana. It had been a while since she heard from anyone in the family. She had decided over a year ago to stop making contact with any of the family and stop sending gifts and cards for birthdays and Christmas. She had helped all of her brothers and sisters out of financial jams at one time or another. She paid their rent, purchased food, clothing or whatever else they needed. She also prevented her father's home from foreclosure. When she got married she purchased clothing for the family and put them up in hotels and gave them money.

Yet she never felt that she was accepted as a sibling.

All those years her father did not believe she was his child and when it was proven by the birthmark she shared, he still did not seem to accept her into the family. Her father just did not care about what he had done and she also felt that her mother did not care enough to show proof of who she was because she must have seen the birthmark on her and her father and compared them.

As an adult, she tried so hard to keep in touch with her family, by calling, sending cards and gifts on special days, visiting and acknowledging the birth of her nieces and nephews.

Also when each one of her children were born she sent family pictures along with their newborn. She never received a response from her family. She received so many beautiful responses from others such as (I am happy for you) (Good luck) (If you ever need a sitter, just give me a call) (Thank you for making me a part of your family) and so many other comments. The only time they saw her children was when she took them over for a short visit. She wanted her children to know their relatives.

On occasions Ruthie would go to some of their functions, but was never introduced as their sister. Most times she would stay for a short time because she did not like what was going on. She did not feel that they missed her nor realized she had left.

After the cold treatment from her father when he found out she was his daughter, she thought he would have been happy but it seemed like he felt "Oh, well" she's my daughter.

When Troy came to pick her up, she cried and never said another word. At that point she decided that she would no longer make a concerted effort to contact her family. If they wanted her they would have to be the ones to contact her. They all knew she was expecting a set of twins.

"Oh, hi Lana." She hesitated to ask how are you doing or anyone else.

"Ruthie, we haven heard from you in quite a while?"

"Oh yes, I am busy with my children and husband, you know they are most important, and my days are filled. They are my life, I have no one else."

"You have us."

"I didn't think so because you all treat me like an outsider. Not one of you acknowledges my family even when I sent you notices of their birth and the growth of our family, over the years. I have tried to acknowledge all of you and your children but, what can I say. My Dad kicked me out and my mother allowed it. My sisters and brothers never included me in anything.

You guys had a mother and father. What did I have? Foster care where I had to fight off someone trying to rape me, an old man constantly trying to break into my room, having to work and buy my own food, living in a home wondering if we had any heat in the dead of Winter and not just once. I was fortunate to have one Foster Care set of parents who wanted to adopt me, but Daddy would not sign the papers because he thought they were too old and if they died he would have to take me home. Well I might add, she died in an airplane crash and a week later her husband died of a massive heart attack a week later and Daddy still did not take me home. I was bounced around in shelters and different foster care homes until I turned eighteen and was on my own. One of the homes I was in had two young drug addicts and alcoholics. One night when I came home from work I ended up running away to the Police Station when one of them tried to take advantage of me, we went to court and they lied about me. However when I was examined, the courts knew they were lying."

"Ruthie, I didn't know you went through all that."

"Well, one thing I knew, I had no one to lean on. I called and begged Daddy to let me come home and that fell on dead ears. I was determined to get an education which would support me, so I would never have to depend on anyone for help."

"You are fortunate, you married a rich man. You are lucky."

"No, I did not marry a rich man. We worked together, made plans and followed through with them. I started working at age fourteen and saving money for college. I never used money to buy fancy things, I saved."

"What about a boyfriend?"

"Boyfriend? I didn't waste my time with boyfriends, because I had no intentions of getting married until I established myself."

"Yeh, I bet Troy changed that."

"No, he didn't. He quit me two times because I didn't do what he wanted me to."

"I knew what I wanted for my life and no man would be allowed to change that.

You know I knew that nobody loved me but one thing I knew was that I loved me and I knew what directions I needed to go if I was going to make it. The only thing Troy got from me before we married was a hug and a kiss."

"Weren't you really in love with him?"

"Yes, very much, but if he loved me he would understand my reason. To me love is a two way street."

"Did he understand?"

"No, that was why he quit me."

"Didn't that hurt you?"

"Sure, but I was not going through a rushed marriage because I am carrying a child. Look, I

Feel that we as women must think out-of-the-box, as well as in-the-box-. We as women must learn to love ourselves because if we don't, that moment of weakness will leave us holding the bag for the rest of our lives, before we truly learn what life expects of us and the kind of life we want to live."

"When Troy quit you, did he go out with other women?"

"He said he didn't, but I don't really know. I know he hung out with another girl, but he said she was never a girlfriend. He said he was watching my every move. He showed me a list of every place I went, the times of day and night."

Lana knew Ruthie had helped her out with her children many times and she had not heard from her in almost two years. So she decided to call. She could have used a little help right now, but just listening to Ruthie and all the things she went through, she was too embarrassed to ask. She never knew why Ruthie was taken out of the home until they all found out about the birthmark. One thing she realized is that she really loved her and will begin to become closer to her and she will do a lot of talking to her siblings about such a strong woman they have as a sister. She has eleven children and all of them are doing well.

And the man she married is right by her side in all that she does in the care of their children.

After Lana hung up the phone, Ruthie wondered why she waited so long to call. She invisioned that she wanted something but decided not to ask, after she told her how she felt about the family. Tammy and Taliah, her twin, came in with Troy. He had them outside in the yard. "Baby, I thought you were going to take a nap?"

"I was on the phone."

"OH, who called?"

"My sister, Lana."

"Haven heard from them in a while."

"Is everything alright?"

"Don't know and don't ask."

"Uh, Uh, gotga."

Troy picked Ruthie up and laid her on the couch. "I want you to stay there until I get back."

"No Troy, I have to bake the cake for Casey's birthday tonight and pick up a few things."

"No, no, I have tickets to a show for him and we are all going out for dinner. I am taking my babies to the office with me, so take a nap. Say bye, bye to mommy" Troy walked over, picked Ruthie up and gave her a smothering kiss, smile and left with the twins.

CHAPTER 28

In life it seems like we are all fighting some battle but when we look at Ruthie life she encountered battles, starting at an early age, even before she could pronounce the word 'battle'. There are many people in the same predicament as she but are unable to graft a hold on life. Ruthie was bounced around so much and landed at the Carters. There she found out what love is and was the recipient of it for three years. This was an eye opener for her. She learned about love. She learned how to protect herself. She studied music, excelled in dancing and voice and she learned about life.

After the Carter's death, she took all those skills with her and was able to deal with the various situations she came across.

Ruthie realized that all of mankind is a pattern, they are drawn up and cut out in different ways, but yet much the same way. Some of mankind have tucks and pleats in different places, but their style is mobile. Some are short (short temper) (long) long winded, wide(spread out) all over the place (tucked in various places)stuck up, (wants thing their way)

But we all have most of the same things which makes us mobile. (the same kind of body parts and their functions. Today most of us can learn, if we choose to. Mankind is a model for imitation and making life work for us. We artistically design life the way we want it to go. Most times it is formed based around how life is seen by us. We know patterns come in many pieces and must be put together and shaped according to our designs and styles. If our design requires a little more and we do not have all we need before we go out and purchase what we need we will take from another (steal). It's almost like a person who is too lazy to work for a living; they tend to rob another and risk being incarcerated.

Ruthie's pattern for life was straight lined. She wondered about others and realized that they were not following the order in which life should go. So many went out of their way to deviate from the way she was treated. She took the correct measurements, pin things down, cut things out, nipped the corners in the right places, stitched and pressed.

When Troy tried to pressure her she stuck to her pattern of life and he got angry, she felt sad for him but did not waste a lot of time crying. She picked up her tools and continued to move forward and never looked back. She felt somewhat bad because she thought he was sincere. Sure she loved him but why spend time loving someone who demonstrated he did not care about your feelings. She was not weakened by that experience, she was strengthened by his actions. When Troy came back into her life, he found out that she was the same, she had not changed to benefit him. Her pattern for her life was still the same and it stayed that way until they got married. He, as a man, learned to respect her wishes and accept her as she was.

Given it is never an option with questioning your choice.

Later on we found that when Ruthie questioned marriage versus Medical school are becoming a mother and a wife, she made the choice she felt was best for her and she might find more happiness. Her trusting belief in herself that becoming a wife and mother would be more fitting than to spend eight years in medical school may be a waste. She had so much

Love to give. Ruthie thought about all the love she had not received can be given to her and Troy's children. She became Doctor Mom, teacher and wife to her family and loved every moment of it.

After Lana called that day and she told her how she felt, her other sisters and brothers began to call and visit her from time to time. Their children were all grown up and some about the same age as Ruthie's. Their children were not as educational oriented as Ruthie's. They tried hanging out together. Troy became a little more open with them. He hired a few of them in his company. He gave them a good talk too before he agreed to any job. They were able to agree with him and take some college classes that he recommended. As they completed the classes they would be moved up to better positions at a hire salary.

Every once in a while Ruthie's sister or brothers would need a little help and they would pay them back. Troy took them off his 'Black List'. Once in a while Ruthie's sisters or brothers would sleep over but Troy did not encourage them to stay. Carrie was the only person who he did not mind sleeping over, she had a key to their house as well as all their children.

Lana was Ruthie's oldest sister and she would come more often and stay over but Troy put a stop to that because it was becoming a habit. She wanted to start bringing friends. Troy would tell her no we are not having anyone sleeping over. Ruthie's father never made a concerted effort to visit and she did not make a concerted effort to call or visit. She accepted the fact that he did not care and no longer worried who she was. It did not bother her if her sisters and brothers came around because she knew if she had not said anything they still would have stayed their distance. They only came around to eat, swim or just chat or play in their game room. Troy did not want just anybody in his pool.

Ruthie's brother became a bit complacent. He thought he could do whatever he wanted. He came to Ruthie's house and brought a friend with him. Troy was not at home, but when he got home and walked in and was introduced to him, Troy was so angry, he came close to telling them to leave. Ruthie walked in. "Hi, Honey, you came back early."

"Yes, I am glad I did." Ruthie saw that look in his eyes and knew he was angry. She knew how jealous he was. Troy rarely brought men around their house. Sometimes a husband and wife from his job for dinner on rare occasions. Ruthie's brother spoke up.

"Hi, Troy, I want you to meet my friend Stu Bradley, I told him about your game room and he had been on my back to come over and play a few games of pool, I hope you don't mind"

Ruthie squeezed Troy's arm. He looked down at her. He spoke unmeaningful. "Okay a few games, because we have other plans. It's always a good idea to call before you come."

Nonchalantly he led the way to the game room. Troy walked back into the room where Ruthie was. She looked at him as she spoke.

"Honey, what was I to do, slam the door in their face?" Troy took Ruthie in his arms and responded. "Yes, and tell them my husband does not allow men in our home if he is not here."

"Our home, don't I have a say?"

"Well----yes, I just don't want any other men in our house when I am not here, period."

"You can trust me."

"It's just that I don't trust anyone around you. I don't want anyone as much as wanting you

Baby, you belong to me."

"Honey there is no one else in this life I want nor can they change my love for you."

You remember the last time at my parents house, up in my bedroom, when I asked you to marry me and you said yes. I was in a state of shock because you had refused me so many times. I almost cried. I was so unhappy. When you told me another time that you were no longer interested in getting married, I felt like crying. I knew then I had to apply more pressure. Then you agree to be my girlfriend. Then I had a chance to work on changing your mind. Baby you don't know the pressure you put me through. I loved you so much. There was no other woman in the world I could see myself with. You know something? You have always had everything in a woman I wanted. I have seen many women and none of them ever measured up to you. Smiling with a chuckle. I believe "GOD" made you for me and I don;t want anyone to interfere with "HIS" decision."

CHAPTER 29

L aying in bed, in Troy's arms, Ruthie's thoughts were about how much she was loved and how much she loved Troy. She thought about her unprecedented life many years ago and who taught her how to love and the efforts she had to put in to pursue a meaningful life. Her thoughts reflected on the Carters.

Mr. and Mrs. Carters were educators before they retired. Both of them loved children and wanted them. Mrs Carter gave birth to two children which only live to the age of two. They were born with some strange illness which could not be treated, so they decided not to try a third time. They became active in anything dealing with children, while they were working in the school system and more so after they retired. After retirement, Mrs Carter volunteered often in the school system providing aid to children with issues intervening their learning and growth. Sometimes she would lecture on various subjects such as homelessness, eating habits, abuse, hunger, bullying or whatever a teacher may suggest.

Mrs. Carter's first encounter with Ruthie was at one of her discussions. She asked for comments and or questions after one of her presentations. She informed the students that she would return in two weeks to respond to their comments, and questions. Going over the comments and questions given by the students, she picked up on Ruthie's. She asked "what is love?".

"Why do parents hate one child and love the other?" "What can a child do to make their parents love them when they never did what they accused them of?" Those questions brought tears to Mrs. Carter's eyes. She had to share it with Mr. Carter. He too was touched by it. Mr. Carter felt that if a child asked questions like this, they were being truthful.

Mrs. Carter brought the comments to Ruthie's teacher for her to read and asked if it would be alright for her to talk to her personally. She agreed and told her that Ruthie was in foster care, her parents had some issues but none of them reflected her behavior or school work in the school. "Ruthie seems to be a very bright girl." She obeys all our rules and stays to herself most of the time with a book or pen and tablet. She is very polite and I have never seen her angry, nor out of character. I noticed that if she sees a student struggling with a problem she will help them out.

After the presentation Mrs. Carter asked a few students to remain. She wanted to comment on their questions and comments they were concerned with from the previous meeting. Then she spoke to Ruthie. Ruthie discussed her comments and questions. Mrs. Carter had a deep sense of concern for what Ruthie was being faced with. Mr and Mrs Carter had talked about foster care and adoption, over a period of time but never put forth the effort to apply. They were financially secured, owned their own home, had a good savings, a very good pension and they were living off of one pension check and their other money went into their savings. Also most of their family members had no financial problems. They themselves were very recognizable and upstanding community people. They completed their application for the Foster care program. Ruthie was living with the Peterson family. She had her duties there. She had to babysit a six month old, wash dishes and she had other household duties as needed. There were another three year old and a fourteen year old boy that stayed sometimes. Mrs. Peterson's nephew. Ruthie lived there about four month and only saw him three times. It seemed like he gave his mother a hard time and Mrs Peterson could do more with him when he got out of hand at his mothers' home. She came home from school one day and no one was home except Rollen, Mrs. Peterson's nephew. Just when she went into her room to change her clothes He walked in. She felt a little frightened the way he was looking at her. "Please leave my room."

"Why? I want to watch you change your clothes."

"If you don't leave right now I am going to call your Aunt."

"She's not here, so call and see where it gets you."

"Okay, you stay, I'll go outside and sit on the steps until she gets home."

"You are not going anywhere but on that bed."

He reached for Ruthie, she gave him a push and he fell over a chair. Ruthie ran out the house, about three blocks down to the police station. She told them what happened, they went to the house and picked him up. Of course, he denied trying to attack her and Mrs Peterson was angry with Ruthie. She walked over to Ruthie and grabbed her arm. "Come on Ruthie, let's go home, nobody's going to bother you." Ruthie looked over at the Officer.

"I am not going back there. Please call my dad and see if I can come home. Please? I am not going with Mrs. Peterson, if you take me there, I will leave. I am not going back there, he tried to take my clothes off." Mrs. Peterson was angry and fired back. "Officer, it's no need to call her father because he is the person who put her out of their home. Do you know why she is here with me, because he put her here. Ruthie you just get your little self together and let's go home. I will call your case worker."

No ma'am, I will not go back to your house." Ruthie looked at the Officer and said. "Please call my case worker as tears continued to scream down her face. Please call Mrs. Leys, she will come get me." She gave them the name and number and Mrs. Leys was there within an hour. Ruthie explained to her what happened. Mrs. Leys believed Ruthie. She took her to the Peterson home to pick up her things and took her to the Shelter until she could find a home for her.

Before they left the Police Station they wanted to know if Ruthie wanted to press charges against Rollen, she told them no because he didn't get to do what he tried. Ruthie told Rollen. Rollen, why don't you wait until you are old enough to have a wife and don't be trying to force yourself on girls, I don't want any babies by someone like you or anyone else until I get married."

Mrs. Peterson broke the Foster Care rules. She was not supposed to have any boys living in her home his age around girls Ruthie's age.

Mrs. Leys, remembered the Carter's, questions concerning Ruthie. The following day she called them. "Hello Mrs. Carter, I was just wondering, did you get all your paperwork in, because I have a young lady who needs shelter. I believe you asked me about her a couple weeks ago."

"Is it the young lady named Ruthie Warren?"

"Yes, that's the one. You mean I can have her?"

"Yes, I had to take her out of another home yesterday."

"Wonderful, when can I pick her up?"

"Well, I have some paperwork to do on her, I will bring her out to you in a day or so."

"Great, I will get her room ready."

Right away the Carters fell in love with Ruthie. She was every kind of person a young girl should be. She was obedient, easy to get along with, very teachable, , when given instructions, followed them with no problem.

After what happened at the Petersons, Mr. Carter set her up for a self defense class. One day Mrs. Carter walked in and Ruthie was playing a song on the piano so she asked if she wanted to start taking lessons. In church she became one of the lead singers in the church choir. The church also had a spiritual dance group, soon she excelled and became one of the trainers. Ruthie became a jewel in the Carters' life.

She was always busy doing many positive things. The Carters were proud of her and the positive efforts she put forth. They tried to adopt her but something always put a block in their way. All the money they received for her care, they put it in a savings account for her. Unknown to Ruthie, the Carters planned for her future. Just in case something happened to them they went to a lawyer and told him to keep track of her and when she finishes high school, make sure she gets the money they had saved for her. Ruthie did not know anything about the savings account until she finished High school. If she needs any direction make sure she is sent to someone who can help her.

Mrs Carter instructed Ruthie to keep in contact with her family, even if they do not reciprocate. "Honey, always acknowledge your family on special occasions even if they do not contact you. Someday they will find the real you. Never allow hate a place in your thoughts, mind or actions. Fill your mind and life with love. Show love in everything you can, Think and plan your life goals. When you set your goals for life, don't allow anyone to change them. If you decide or have questions about a goal change, make sure it's going to benefit you. Your first love should be for the "CREATOR' and then ourselves. Never feel sorry for anyone, just reach out and help if you can. Remember, we all came from the same "CREATOR" and each of us has the opportunities to excel. Some of us may have to struggle much more than others, but still could make it if we tried.

CHAPTER 30

●••••••••••••••••••••••••••••••••••••●

Troy was the oldest child of the Thompsons and the only one for ten years. He never wanted for anything. Mr. and Mrs. Thompson were not rich by any means but they never suffered for anything. They worked at fairly decent jobs which enabled them to pay their bills on time and they always had a little left over to add to their savings. Troy always got everything he wanted and he got his way at all times with his parents. They loved him very much and he loved them. He was never a bad child and the things he wanted were not out of his parents reach, financially. Two years before he was old enough to drive a car he went to a Car Show with his father and he saw a car he wanted, which was popular with guys at that time and the cost was almost twice as much as his fathers' and the day of his birthday his father took him to the dealer to pick it up. That was the biggest surprise of his life. He was well sought after by the girls and many of the guys wanted to be friends with him so they could take their girl for a drive in his car. The Thompsons' didn't think any girl was good enough for Troy. His mother would try talking him out of any girl she didn't like. She would always find a reason to show a dislike for a girl. She was not pretty enough, too skinny, too fat, hair too short, you name it she would develop a dislike, if Troy was getting too close. When Susan came along, she kept Troy close. His duty was to help out with her if a need arises, as a sitter. Troy didn't want to give up chances of getting the things he wanted. When his mother wanted him to babysit, he was right there for her. It didn't matter if he had to break a date because he could always get another. Mrs. Thompson did not want him attached to any girl for too long, if he did she would find something wrong with her which would encourage Troy to stop bringing her around. Troy's life was like a whirlwind; it kept moving in different directions.

Mrs Thompson was kind of glad when Ruthie moved in, because as much as she knew about her background it did not measure up to theirs. She tried to instill that into Troy. She was pleased with the help and encouragement she brought in her home which helped her daughters, especially Carrie. Susan was also overly fond of her and the help she gave her, as well. Ruthie helped her to understand how important education is and it helped her to change her perspectives and started working a little harder at bringing up her grades. Susan was quite frustrated with her parents and the controls they were placing on her. Ruthie discussed the importance of parents and abiding by their rules. She also talked about standing firm on what you believe is best for you and comparing that with what's available to you and the way you want your life to go at the time, then determine what would be the best directions for you to take.

When they talked about college, Susan stated that she planned to go as far away as possible. Ruthie never thought how serious Susan was.

"Susan, why don't you attend college right here? You will be able to walk, have a place to stay, and not have to worry about food?

"Oh, no Ruthie, I cannot take my parents any longer, they are not going to control me like my brother."

"But Susan, if you go too far, look at what you have to deal with, a place to live, food, transportation, clothing, a job? At home these things will be taken care of."

"That's okay, I am willing to take the challenge."

"Susan, your parents love you very much and they want the best for you, it's there way of showing their love."

"No Ruthie, it's their way of trying to control your life, their way. All they have to do is give me the same amount that they gave my brother and I will earn the rest. I am not afraid of work."

"Well Susan, I want you to know I am always here for you, if you need anything. Just give me a call. I will always be your friend. I always had one friend, since I was seven years old who believed in me and knew that I was honest in all my dealings. When I had a problem, she stood up for me and by me.

When Ruthie moved into the Thompsons apartment, Mrs Thompson did not see her as someone Troy would fall in love with. She had no roots in the City. Although she was a beautiful girl, attending college and started to work at a local Doctor's office. All that did not matter nor did it bring up her social standards in the community. She felt that she could be someone Troy could play around with or sleep over some nights and nobody would know about the little connections.

The little connections Ruthie had with Troy, to her he felt like a brother to her and Carrie and Susan sisters. Troy asked her to go to some games with him and other times the movies but she always had something else to do. She did not want a close relationship with anyone at this time. She did not want to meet his girlfriend, nor hang out with him and his friends. Troy had become attractive to her and was trying to build a relationship but she did not know it.

Something about him began to change. He seems to stare at her from time to time. She had an uneasy feeling around him. Ruthie stopped going into the house when he was there.

Ruthie can never forget Bob Brene and the way he stared at her, before the attack.

She believed his mother noticed the change in him when she was around, because she began to act a little different toward her. She could not pinpoint how are what but she knew something was going on in Troy's mind and his parents. She would always help the girls with their school work when the need be when they asked.

Troy wasn't bringing any girls around anymore. He would offer Ruthie rides to the campus whenever he saw her start out. At first she accepted, then she started refusing. "Oh, it's a nice day I would rather walk, thanks anyway" She could tell he got a little angry. Mrs Thompson questioned her reason for not accepting a ride later that day.

"Mrs Thompson, I do not mind walking and I like to walk because I was early for class."

"Well, when it gets cold, you will welcome a ride."

"I suppose that will be another one of my challenges, I will have to face."

When Carrie was giving Troy a hard time, he asked Ruthie to come and talk to her. Troy

Saw his chance to offer to take her to a movie. She accepted but wanted to take Carrie. He was disappointed but on conditions that she go for a ride after taking Carrie home. He was pleased when she agreed. At the Club he told Ruthie he was in love with her and wanted to get married right away. Ruthie refused his advancement. He did not pressure her but it gave her a lot to think about.

On their second date, he tried to apply more pressure. He wanted to set a wedding date and try enough pressure for her to allow him to stay overnight. He was somewhat angry and wanted her to go away with him to a business conference. She agreed if she could have her own room. He agreed that she would have her own room. However at the conference he tried to stay in her room and she refused. They were the only two people with a single room. All the others (wives and significant others)shared the same room. Troy was embarrassed and angry. He forced himself in Ruthie's room for the last night they were there. He slept in the bed and Ruthie on a chair. She refused to get in bed with him. That morning he gave her fifteen minute to get ready or find her way home. He left and she found her way home. After that day Ruthie started looking for another place to live. When he told his mother what happened she asked Ruthie to find another place to live because she was going to raise the rent. Ruthie's plans were already in progress. She moved a few days later. Carrie and Susan were very upset. Troy was upset when Ruthie moved and very angry with his mother for suggesting it. He found out where she moved and was keeping a record of where she went unknowing to Ruthie. He wanted to make sure she was not going out with any other guys. He was angry with himself for the way he treated her. He was so much in love with her. He thought of a hundred ways to try and get her back but was afraid to approach her. He tried to get Susan and Carrie to tell her to come over and help them with a project but they refused because he was the reason she was not there.

After Ruthie and Troy got married and had six children his parents became ill and needed someone to help care for them. They could afford to pay some outside helper but they felt that their children should be the ones to provide the help they needed. The Thompson lured Troy over as often as they could. Troy was so mixed up between helping his parents and being there with his wife and children. He started drinking heavily and staying with his parents. He would go to work, sometimes come home and most times go to his parents. His mother would keep him a good supply of liquor. When it runs low she would order more.

She felt that she was punishing Ruthie for having so many children and taking her son away. Also she felt it was Ruthie's fault that her children were not as close to her and there to take care of them. She even encouraged Troy to divorce Ruthie and move in completely with them.

What brought Troy to his senses Ruthie had agreed to get married to a Doctor who was willing to take her and all her six children into his home. He went to him and told him, there is nobody going to marry my wife but me. His children told him all the things their grandmother had said about their mother and he confronted them.

CHAPTER 31

 ●━━ ●●●●●●●●●●●●●●●●●●●●●●●●●●●● ━━●

Marlo kept Ruthie abreast of her progress. She found a job based on the training she took. She made a good salary and no longer had to depend on the Welfare System. Also she had expected to receive about seventy five thousand dollars as a result of some property left to her and a brother from their grandparents and some insurance money from a policy found on their parents after the death of their parents which was never paid to anyone. The policy was paid in full, which was found among some papers, by her brother. Marlo didn't know very much about her family because of the way her parents lived. She told Ruthie she wanted to pay her back all the money she owed her, but Ruthie told her to put it in a savings account, for Timmy. All she wanted was for her and Timmy to take her out for dinner when they got the time. Marlo. ' salary was so that they were able to move into a larger apartment so Timmy could have his own room. Marlo told Ruthie that when she gets the money she will be buying a car because at this time she had to depend on a bus and that was very inconvenient traveling when the weather was bad.

She had to tell Ruthie about the people she worked with. She met a nice guy who she was in class with and so happened they both got a job at the same place. Ruthie was happy to hear that she met someone she seemed to like.

"Oh, that's nice."

"Ruthie, I think he likes me. He is so helpful at work, since we do the same things on the job, sometimes there are things I don't know, he helps me out and I do the same for him. He asked me out to dinner. Do you think I should go?"

"Sure, why not?"

"Okay, I am going to say yes and Timmy must be able to come as well."

"That's a good idea."

"My problem is, two guys have asked me out and I am not sure which one to say yes to."

"Why don't you try the one who wants to take you to a family place. Let them know you have a son and he must come with you."

"I don't want to be stepping on any other women's man. I don't want another Tom."

"Have you heard from Tom lately?"

"Oh, yes, you know his wife had a set of twins and one of them is severely mentally challenged. I didn't know that until I saw them in the Mall. She didn't see me. They looked to be about four years old. The little boy looks just like Timmy. If I hadn't given birth to Timmy, I would swear Timmy belonged to them. Ruthie I was shocked. Also the Lady from Welfare called me to let me know Tom was trying to find my address and she told him I was no longer in need of their services and they did not know."

"I am glad you are not in that City any longer."

"But you know Ruthie I have to get in touch with the Brenes, because I believe I left some important papers there. My Aunt gave them to me some years ago and told me to always keep them with me in an important place. I remember having them at the Brenes. I believe I left them up in that closet in the room we stayed in. I need those papers, I think they are my parents birth certificates and marriage records. I dread going over there are calling them, but I must. Do you think you can take me over there one day, anytime convenient for you?

"Sure, can it be on a weekend?".

"Anytime you say."

"Give Timmy a big hug for me."

"Will do, and thanks."

CHAPTER 32

Tom came by his mother's house to see if she would watch his son. Mrs. Brene never liked to watch him because he was so much trouble. They never took the time to train him and never fed him on a timely basis. He always messes himself up and gives her such a hard time when she tries to clean him up.

When she saw Tom's car in the yard she took her time going inside. Tom and Bob was so busy reminiscing they did not hear her come in.

"You know Bob when Mom had those girls here, I had so much fun. That Marlo was so easy, I could get her to do anything and she even lied for me."

"Yeah man, you got off easy but Ruthie would not budge. That night she got me so mad, I was going to bash her head in. She was a fighter. I started to rip every piece of clothes off her, but she brought her knee up in my stomach and thought I was done for life. Somebody taught her some self defense. "Tom chuckled," I wonder what she's doing now?"

"I saw a glimpse of her on TV the other day, she was helping with some Community activities where she lives. You know she can really sing and she still looks good. Man, I wanted her."

"Marlo was a piece - of- crap, anything goes with her and she came back here thinking I would marry her. She gave me what I wanted when I wanted it. Who did she think I was. Mom didn't want us to marry trash."

Mrs. Brene could not allow herself to listen any more.

Boys, I am ashamed of you, You mean to tell me I stood up for you, for all the wrong reasons. I loved you guys but, do you mean they were being honest and I was wrong. You were the abusers? Those girls did not have parents who stood up for them, they did not have parents who cared about them, they did not deserve to be abused. They kept their mouths shut so they could have a place to stay and I could have money to feed you and we all could have a place to live. How could you do such a thing behind my back. I am ashamed of the things I said to them and about them. I am hurt because you could have been in the same predicament, if it wasn't for them. I taught you guys to never look down at anyone, to always look across at them and if you cannot help them do nothing to harm them.

Look at Ruthie, she did so much to build up our church, with the young people and many of them are still there today. She was so quiet and real, she never bothered anyone. She alway lifts others up.

Although Marlo was different, she would do anything to please others. Marlo called me that day when you left Tom. Her rent money left as well and acted very natively, now I am beginning to think how wrong I was. If a man steals from his child and causes him to become homeless, what kind of man is he? That girl was on a month to month lease and if her rent was not paid on time she had three day to get out. That girl had lost her job because she had to stay home and take care of her sick child. Marlo willingly gave herself to you and you should have willingly helped care for that child. Let's not forget you except what she gave you.

I am so ashamed of you guys and myself. That little boy is my grandson and I should be doing more for him. Right now I am sick and discussed with myself." Tom looked over at Bob as he spoke. "I guess Mom's right, I never looked at those girls like that. I am going to try and find out where Marlo's is and help out more with Timmy."

"Yeah Tim, I guess we were wrong, because you know Ruthie could had brought charges and I would have been branded for the rest of my life, She told the court that her top was torned in the process and she herself downplay the attempt rape. Man I could have gone to prison

CHAPTER 33

Chris Warren and his wife Gloria were both getting up in age and no longer able to totally care for themselves. He turned his house over to his son, in hope that he would provide the necessary care for them. Once he did that his son was having parties almost every weekend.

Drinking and loud music and crowds and it was difficult for them to get any rest. Mr. Warren thought about Ruthie and that big house they had and that most of their children are out on their own. He thought that would be the perfect place to live. He felt bad about the way he had treated her and she had still done so much for him and her sisters and brothers. He wanted to apologize but was too embarrassed to know how. What was I thinking? She was a baby, Why didn't he just such-it-up and care for her like any other child? Before he attempted to ask for forgiveness he chose to just stay away and have no contact with her. He could not undo what he did. If by some chance Ruthie would call him then that would open the door for him to let her know how sorry he was. He forbade Gloria to call.

Chris Warren realized how much he hurt the women he was so crazy in love with and how much she loved him, knowing that Ruthie was his child but went along with him in casting her out of their home. He thought about the children he raised, watched them grow up, fed them, clothes them, sent them to school, got them out of trouble and now he turned his house over to them and cannot get a good night's rest and now his son wants to put them in a Nursing Home. They are not totally disabled. They can prepare their own meals, shop, and clean up behind themselves. It's just that they don't drive.

CHAPTER 34

Ruthie's brother Stewart came to Her and asked if could take their father and Gloria in to live with them. Realizing that Ruthie was home most of the time because Troy did not allow her to be roaming around out and about. He was too jealous for that. He knew most of the children were married, in college or have their own place. He knew they had many empty rooms. He didn't want the responsibility of caring for his parents. He knew they did not need total care. Ruthie talked to Troy and decided that they could stay for a month.

Ruthie felt that her father was not man enough to come to her but without any wordiness she just left everything unsaid.

One evening while they were all sitting in the family room Mr. Warren started the conversation.

"I don't know how to apologize for the many things you went through because of the decisions I made. I have searched myself many times, wondering why I did the things I did. That's why I have not been calling you because I just did not know where to begin. I must say that you have been more of a daughter to me than any of the others. You have given and not asked for anything in return. You were there for me in my sickness and made sure everything went well, you have bailed me out when I was about to lose my home. I have signed my home over to the wrong person. I must say as soon as I signed it over to my son he wanted to put us in a Nursing Home or dump us on you or one of the other kids who are barely surviving themselves. There is a saying that 'the one you do the least for, will do the most for you in a time of need'. I want you to know Gloria and I thank you for the time we will be here. Your home will be like a vacation for us. No drinking and cussing, no loud music, no sleepless night. Life is wonderful when you know you are loved. I can see that all of your children are loved and I see no jealousy, they are respectful, kind to each other, smart and moving up in the world. You got Doctors, Lawyers, Nurses, Businessmen and Women. How you managed that the way the world is today.

"Well Dad, I think it's love, respect and drive. All our children are our favorite and special. None is no better than the others. Our children know that Troy and I love each other very much and we love them as well. We do not try to hold them at home, we encourage them to get an education and move up and out. If need be our home and doors are always opened and each of them have keys. Love has everything to do with parenting. Our children are not allowed to degrade one another or talk back to us. They were taught to talk to us early in life.

Children have to be taught from the cradle. It's never cute when they hit you or spit on you or go berserk when they do not get their way. Those are teaching moments and ways to show your love.

CHAPTER 35

● ·························· ●

Children should not have to be responsible for the care of their parents in their old age.

They can do so if they agree. Parents should establish these concerns during their lifetime. Children have their own family. Why should they have to take this responsible. Things like this could cause a breakup between a husband and wife. He or she did not marry one's mother and father. Parents should prepare for life after retirement. Suppose the husband's parents become ill and the wife's parents become ill and the husband and wife have three or four small children and just surviving, What are the children to do? The care they need cannot be provided by the children, and it's not because they do not love them, it's because they are unable to. Early in life parents should get a designated person to handle their affairs if they become ill so they do not have to have sisters and brothers blaming each other because they are not doing their part. We all should have some sort of senior care insurance to cover the expenses in a facility when we as seniors cannot care for ourselves. Sure it can be costly but what is it costing your children if it may be the breakup of their marriage.

Love your children, don't place pressures on them.

This book covers many issues which can happen in life. Think about them and see which ones you can identify with. Determine the outcome and think about what you would have done if you were faced with any of them.

Some parts of these things actually happened but the story was built around to add other things to show what might have been a good outcome.

Life is built around love, hate, trial and tribulation but, in life love should be the dominant consideration in all we do and try to do. It shouldn't be filled with tears.

We must never give up on anything about life, but keep it in your thoughts and move on to the next things. It's good to reflect back from time to time to see if any additional information developed but move forward. We are growing older each day but constantly reflecting back in the past. Let's move forward because life is filled with love.

Ruthie thought about her life before and after she met Troy. She felt that her life was meant to be troublesome because it led her to the love of her life. In all the problems existed, she managed to protect and overcome them. She was provided with everything she needed to withstand what she endured. She had a mindset which gave her the strength to deal with the issues in her life. She never labeled the whys? She moved forward on the things which she could accomplish and concerned herself with. Ruthie continuously prepared herself for a future. She did not hold grudges and tried not to allow hate to burden her. She remembered the good times and those who loved her. The Brenes boys were not going to control her, The Crossleys she just had to always be aware of the Mister. Her family, she tried to keep in contact, She was not aware of why her father did the things he did and now she know. She can forgive him because there is one thing, you cannot change is the pass. She thought, if he had not done what he did she most likely would not have met Troy. Troy was her first, last and only love of her life. She gave birth to eleven children and now they have many grand- children and sons and daughter in laws and they are also the love of their life. She and Troy are as much in love as they were from the beginning. We might ask "What's Love Got to do with it?" The answer is "Everything".

CHAPTER 36

If we are a person who believe in "THE CREATION" Let's think about Jesus Christ. He did not have to become born like man and come to earth, suffer and die like he did, for us.

However, because He love us, His sisters and brothers, He did. He believed in us. He wanted us to know if we made mistakes, we could be forgiven, if we choose too, But we much asked for forgiven and truly be honest about it. We must start living a true and honest life. We must stand firm and live right by studying "GOD'S word. Hate should not be apart of our thoughts.

We must treat everyone with respect. If you do not like what someone is doing are the things they do, or how they perceive you, there is nothing saying you have to remain constantly in their presents. There is no one that can force you to do what they are doing, by comforting you. You do not have to do what your so-call friends are doing, just because you think they are your friends. Friends do not cause harm to friends. Friends do not suggest you do wrong.

Friends cannot live your life. Nor does love suggest you to do wrong. But one thing we all will learn is that lust will lead you in the wrong direction. Immediate desires will make suggestions for you but one must refrain from lust and stay away from cozy dark places which may cause these kinds of feelings. Let's not involve ourselves in moments which will cause us a lifetime of struggles. It, all, only, requires us to think before we act and that only takes a moment before we act.

Our lives will and can last a very long time without so much heartache, if we only take the time to think of the outcomes of what we do and what may happen. Ruthie Warren was one who saw how she wanted her life to be and she knew how and when to put the controls into action. Sure the desires to make changes was there but she had a good idea what might happen so she chose to do it her way and later in life the love and respect for herself paid off.

Even though she thought she had lost it. When we stand firm on what life has to offer, most times things will workout better for us. Things may not always be as we want them to be, just much better than we had in mind.

We tend to seek things from others that they are not capable of providing. Even our parents, many times lack the ability to show the love that we need, yet we can see it given to a sibling.

This you can provide for your children on and even scale.

We can take a deep look at Marlo and how she treated Ruthie. Ruthie did not blame her because she understood Marlo's reasoning. Marlo did not understand, she thought those guys and that home was a safe haven for her. When she got into trouble, she called on the only person she thought could help her and she did.

Early in life Ruthie felt and experienced so much unloved and she saw what love was and how it worked so she built her life around what it means. She took notes from the various homes she was placed in and began to form her solution. She used the libraries as her study hall.

She realized that education was her main tools and number one goal was to be able to care for her self. This was her starting point for life.

Ruthie loved life and everyone she came in contact with. She knew everybody did not love her but, what did she care? That was okay. She found out about the "Creator" and that He was our Heaven Father and we were all sisters and brother. That was enough for her. Studied the scriptures and attended church when she could. She did not merely listen to the Ministers in the Churches, she studied and even questioned them at time and formed her own reasoning. She merely just did not go along with the way they taught. She formed her own conclusions at times. Sunday was not the only sabbath day, every day should be lived righteously. She always lived with the thoughts that if no one else cared about her. "Heavenly Father" did. Living with the Carter" s was a place that she felt she was placed by "GOD" because this was where she really was prepared for life. The time she was there she felt that her life of learning began. Even though, her desire for learning had already been established

By other means. In life we are unsure why we land in certain places, but if we begin to work within where we are placed and positive things begin to happen, then we know we are at our starting points in life. We must begin to start building our lives and see where it leads us. We all know right from wrong because we will get a positive or negative feeling in what we are doing. Life is beautiful and can be enjoyable when doing the right things. There is so much beauty around us to enjoy. GOD has instill in man to establish so much for our enjoyment. We only have to see, feel and capture our enjoyment. Just think, there was a time we had to walk every where, then the wheels were developed. Carts came along, horses, wagons, cars, boats, airplanes and so on. Then listing devices, TV's, telephones, cell phones and so on.

The bookends here, but life continuously is moving on in many directions. We only must follow and use the pattern we chose. The tools we need are all around us.